Loving Legit

A novel

by **Serena King**

Real love begins at home …

King Publishing
P.O. Box 920556
Norcross, GA 30010

ISBN: 978-0-9862125-0-5

Printed in the United States of America

This book is dedicated to every woman looking for a good man, a legit man.

Table of Contents

Preface

This story is about a good woman who wants nothing more than to find a good, honest man. We have all been there, haven't we, ladies? And we know how hard that can be.

Sometimes the disadvantage in being female is that you don't understand the ways of men, and *if* a woman's been hurt time and time again, she won't know who's for her and who's not. Maybe she's too busy blinding herself with "bad-man radar habits" from the past. Maybe she didn't grow up with great examples of "legit" men, so the guys she goes for, and who are attracted to her, are the ones who arrive because she's vulnerable, unsure of herself, desperate, and—most of all—doesn't realize what she truly deserves.

Sometimes, women are even attracting guys who are mirror images of themselves, and they don't even know it. Think about that. Is she honest with herself? Does she even know who she is internally? What about her limits: how far has she pushed herself into being dishonest or behaving in a way that wasn't satisfactory, and then expected a mate who would show her anything more than what she was capable of giving in return? Does she truly trust herself, and if she doesn't, how can she attract a mate who brings forth that quality? If the man is weak and the woman is weak, now there are two weak beings trying to complete one another—an impossibility.

It is time that women take responsibility and correct their own faults. It's time that women stop comparing themselves to video vixens—unrealistic images of themselves featured on magazine covers, or perhaps that exotic woman from another country her ex left her for! We need to celebrate being single and appreciate who we are! Start loving ourselves from deeper within. Women seem to focus so much on being loved and finding a mate that they forget they should be practicing getting closer to a higher power and learning to love themselves.

When you're finally in a relationship or married, do you have what it takes to not lose yourself in the shadows of a man, keeping your individuality while still complementing him? Have you spent so much time looking for a man or trying to keep one, that you've lost yourself? Are you still reading and feeding your brain, hanging with friends, traveling, becoming one with yourself, or is finding a man more important? Are you looking for a man to complete you—or to complement you?

If a guy can't see what a beautiful and rare flower you are, then he may not be the guy for you. Change yourself for no one, but be honest with yourself. If you know there are issues within you that need to be ironed out, admit you're not yet ready for love and do some serious self-evaluating and housecleaning.

Be the beautiful you that you already are! Don't allow a few bad mishaps to ruin the sweetness about you. You know … that sweetness that becomes bitterness when the guy you *thought* was for you proves you were wrong.

Maybe you've proven *yourself* wrong, believing you deserved something you weren't even ready to receive. Make sure you are a whole, healthy, and complete woman before you seek love, and the right one will arrive. Continue on as a happy woman, get your paper up, get a hobby, be helpful to others, and work on your spiritual connections. No one wants to be alone, but don't want to be with someone so badly that you waste years of your life trying to connect with Mr. Wrong.

Maybe he isn't Mr. Wrong. Maybe you're so caught on the past that you push men away, pretend you're someone else to please them, or hang on so tightly that you become unattractive, hard to please, or worse—a convenient placeholder.

Every woman has a special fire about her that burns bright, and men love this, so be patient. Be radiant, because when you don't love, trust, or respect yourself, it shows. That exciting fire about you burns down.

Remember, if there is no communication then there can't possibly be a relationship. If there is no trust, then someone is being dishonest about how she feels and what her true intentions are because that is *not* love. Love *you* first, genuinely care about others, and someday someone will show you a true and real love that you never thought existed.

The story you're about to read narrates the adventures of one Monica Walker. She's a woman I'm sure you'll recognize—you've probably met someone very much like her in the mirror. The story is fiction, but like all fiction, it has its roots in the author's life experiences, so you'll be meeting me in many of these pages. Let's see what happens when a girl who's worldly successful decides to look for the one thing still missing in her life: a great relationship. Will Monica ever find her legit man?

Meet Monica Walker

Have you ever wanted something so bad that you would do just about anything to get it? I mean like, you work for it. You live, eat, crave, and breathe it, because you know that it's the one thing that'll make your life whole again?

Yep, that's me. Monica Walker. I'm the thirty-year-old owner of *Senseless Woman Magazine*. You might wonder why I'd give it such a strange name, but I had my reasons.

Hey, just kidding! The real name of my magazine is *Enterprise 25*. I came up with that because twenty-five marked the year when my life had finally shown me some real meaning, and the enterprise of starting this magazine had been one huge undertaking, let me tell ya'. A lot of sweat, tears, and sacrifice went into making sure this dream became a vibrant reality.

The magazine caters to women aged twenty-five to forty. It covers stories on lifestyle, healthy relationships, and family— of course there are segments with fashion advice, sex advice—pretty much all the basics.

I like to joke that the magazine's title is *Senseless Woman* because for most of my years, I'd been a pretty senseless woman. I was switching jobs every few years and changing cities as often as I'd change clothes.

I came up with the idea for the magazine back in Atlanta and figured I could get the most exposure in New York City. *NEW YORK*, baby! I took the idea and ran with it. I ended up getting a grant for a space, some angel investors, and even had start-up money for a few staff. Eight months later, we were getting ready to launch our second issue. Go figure.

All of that success with just one slight problem, I wanted and needed a man! That was what I longed for in my soul.

My home girls believed I was running away from something, but of course I denied it. They said I switched cities so much mostly because I couldn't find a decent man. Well, now I was in the Big Apple and planned to add a little spunk to my life. New York is a big city, so I was pretty sure the pickings were far and wide.

My home girls are extremely educated, beautiful, successful—and married. I was the only one who didn't have someone to kiss under the mistletoe yet! I didn't know if I was too picky, if my standards were too high, if I was just dealing with the wrong type of men, *OR* if there was something wrong with me.

Can our standards be too high? Come on now, a girl's not just going to pick up the next thug released from prison to bring home to Mama. It just ain't happening!

I wanted a respectable man, one with substance and mystery, and one who knew how to give love as much as all of them liked to receive it.

I was tired of dealing with the half-ass-ness of it all. You know: the ones that like to take you on one date then believe it's an open invite or an all-access pass to get a key to the bedroom.

I even had to cut one guy off because every time we'd go out, he'd bring alcohol. And what guy in his right mind asks a woman does she want to see what his mattress feels like? If that's some odd way of romancing a woman, someone please hand me a dictionary so I may look up what sick and twisted word that definition belongs to.

I assume so many women allow men to get away with this stuff for so long that these guys continue to play the same card with every woman they meet.

How many of us gals haven't engaged in sex outside a relationship just for kicks and giggles? Might as well just throw all our morals and values out the window, because this generation is the most oversexed yet.

One thing's for sure: good men and good women have matured beyond that sort of game playing. They're looking for the same thing. They just need to find each other—someone on the same wave length to be their partner.

Speaking of maturity, I certainly haven't won any medals. My college years were one wild ride, let me tell ya' . . . living the dorm life and dealing with guys whose only objective was to sleep with as many girls as they could, to get more notches on their belt than the next clueless guy!

Guys wanted to dip and dab but not feel obliged to commit. And most girls just went along with it. Are we not deserving of something more than a booty call?

The guys forced us girls to have standards and demand what we wanted. Otherwise we'd wind up being someone's doormat, which is what happened to most of us. This is not to say some girls didn't *want* one-night stands or random hook-up/friendship duos.

But pah-lease. I'm all of thirty, and I need a man, a real man. One that's caring, loving, honest, respectable, spiritual—you know, all that good, mushy stuff. Hell, I'm willing to give it in return, so why not?

Aside from me wanting to find a good man—a legit man, as my home girls call it— let me tell you what led to this whole New York ordeal in the first place.

A Little Backstory

Now I'm originally from St. Louis, Missouri. Not East St. Louis—you know, the area where you can't stop at traffic lights or even dare ask for directions if you're lost. Nope, I'm right from the heart of University City, Missouri. The home of the best Chinese food I've ever tasted! Now you know I can't forget about the Imo's Pizza, White Castle, or the Red Hot Riplet Potato Chips. Man, how I'd *missed* home.

The days of University City basketball games and Hazelwood East skip day . . . none of my friends went to Hazelwood East, nor did I, but they all liked to skip school on "skip day," in order to make it to Six Flags.

They skipped school just to follow around all the guys they thought were cute. I could *NEVER* get away with anything like that. I'd be picking myself up off the floor the minute my mother ever knew I was partaking in such foolishness.

She'd always say things like, "Those little boys don't want anything from you but to get into your pants," or "You have other things to focus on, like college."

Until recently, I never knew why my mother was so strict and stern about those sorts of things. Now that I am of age, I completely understand. It's *TRUE*. Guys are known to think about sex at least eighteen times a day!

Isn't that crazy?

Once they got what they wanted from you, they were sure to leave you broken-hearted, empty, and strung out on what you believed to be love.

I guess that's why the female praying mantis eats half her mate midway through the mating session, and when he's done she eats the rest of him. Talk about a true "man eater."

Half the girls I went to school with had babies by the time I was twenty-four. They were all pretty naive to say the least, allowing some sweaty guy to whisper sweet nothings into their ear until they got turned on enough to get pregnant. Then the guy would just walk away from his responsibility, like he was still a virgin.

That's crazy, right? Having babies?

That was the furthest thing from my mind at that age. I was just finishing college, and after a few years of dealing with college guys, who all reminded me of high school guys who still had milk behind their ears, I couldn't imagine it.

I'd come from a very big family, five sisters and a brother, to be exact. I was separated from them when I was all of nine years old. Those were some very difficult years. My parents were on drugs, and my dad was physically, verbally, and emotionally abusive, so I guess street life had finally caught up to them.

Division of Family Services snatched us up before we ever knew or could understand what was going on. My older brother lived in Detroit with his stepmom, so he wasn't around when all of that was going down. Therefore, that left me as next in charge. The eldest of six girls!

What was I to do? What could I do about my sisters and I being taken?

I was young, clueless about what it meant to be a parent, and scared. Most believe that the system is corrupt and that they'd rather give foster parents funds to care for someone else's children than to actually allow the biological parents to get themselves together.

I guess I could understand why if the parents are marked as unfit, the children living in unhealthy environment and always left without supervision.

Where would my life be now if I hadn't gone through such a tough time?

Anyway, I left high school and entered college shortly after. I'd graduated with a degree in journalism, so now I was running one of the top magazines in New York, and I'd started it! I had beaten the odds by reaching massive success.

What more could a girl ask for? Want, even?

Of course! *A MAN!* I was thirty, and I believed I was too successful, full of spunk, and smart to be alone. I was hormonal, my biological clock was ticking, and I needed to pop some babies out, at least before I hit forty. I had to be kidding myself if I thought that was going to be easy.

I had a pretty long relationship when I was in college, and it went sour. I was madly in love with the guy, but apparently he wasn't feeling the same—not at that time, at least. There was always this nasty back-and-forth thing going on. I don't know if it's because we were so young or what.

A short tale—we met freshman year in college. It was crazy, because I'd randomly seen this guy in a Target store before making it to campus. I didn't pay much attention to him at first, but I'd gotten a quick glimpse of who he was. A little nerdy, but behind his glasses, I saw potential.

When I'd finally made it to campus, I moved in, got settled, and went to an all-white affair, hosted by the alumni association. The event incorporated three colleges—Spelman, Morehouse, and Clark Atlanta University. There were so many students I could barely navigate my way through the crowd! We all wore the same shirts, which called for us to open up and get to know one another. The process was nerve-wrecking.

I was in a new state, nineteen, and clueless about where life would lead me. I didn't recognize a single soul . . . and then it happened.

Out of maybe a few thousand students, I'd spotted him again. I became very relaxed at that point, because I felt like I was seeing someone I knew. It was easier to start a conversation with him since I'd seen him before.

We chatted for a while and mixed and mingled among the other students. By the end of the night, we exchanged phone numbers, and the deal was sealed.

His name was James Harris.

I'd made my very first new friend. I never really thought it would lead to anything more than just a friendship, but it did, and very early on. It happened fast!

I was a little bit of a tomboy growing up, so I always connected well with the guys. As far as me considering James as a love interest, his nerdy glasses and New Balance tennis shoes had to go!

Anyway, most of us knew that college relationships rarely work, but for some reason I felt like this one could. I was quite optimistic. I mean, when I spoke with my elders, they'd always say that you'd possibly meet and marry the love of your life, and you might find him, in college.

However, I was new to all this. I never really had a father to show me the ropes of the dating world, so I was going into this thing like a blind bat! All I had were older female cousins to school me through it, along with a couple of unrealistic images of love—you know, romance novels and movies. Of course, the advice was wise, but a woman's guidance could never replace that of a man's, and I yearned for that. I longed for a father's affection, direction, and instruction.

I'd had a very strict upbringing, so dating was pretty much non-existent in our household. I was a freshman in college, and I'd never *EVEN* been on a real date. Not only that, I spent a great portion of my life watching my biological father physically abuse my mom, doing alcohol and drugs. Talk about a great example of what my future husband should look like.

If getting escorted to the school dances and brought straight home was considered a date, then I guess there you have it. Beyond that—forget it! My foster parents didn't play that!

I'd learned early on, though, that guys didn't want to date. They just wanted to sleep with everything that had legs, breasts, and thighs.

Well, I'd become a victim. I'd lost my virginity at the very tender age of nineteen, to an upper-classmen who I surely didn't end up with. He was a complete jerk.

Years later I found out he'd become a psychiatrist and got married off to some Asian woman.

It seemed as if James would wind up being no different. An afterthought.

James and I, however, remained friends and hung out every so often. We later entered into a relationship, but it was short-lived. He started hanging out with his friends, and his decision-making became tainted. There was always another girl—I was constantly in tears.

I knew he probably no longer want to be with me, but we just kept holding on. It was convenient, you know? We finally broke it off and decided to go our separate ways.

Soon after, when sophomore year rolled around, it was time for applying for internships and figuring out what would soon become of us, as we went out to make our names in the work force.

As friends, James and I stayed close, and we were always updating one another on our level of success. He was interning in New York that summer, and I was headed back home to St. Louis for work.

I wished James well on his adventure as he took off. When in St. Louis, he'd call, and we stayed in touch that summer. We made the executive decision to meet up a few times while he was away.

I booked my flight and headed to New York to see him. Man, did I have a great time. He showed me all the great tourist attractions. We ate pizza until my face gleamed of zits from all of the grease, but most importantly, we rekindled our romantic relationship.

That was until he butt-dialed me and I overheard an entire conversation he was having with some chick he'd gone on a date with.

Months later he confessed to having a one-night stand. The chick had managed to rack up a hundred-dollar meal, so I guess he felt he had to get something out of that deal.

After the summer ended, it was time to return to school in Atlanta, and I was ready to go. Entering into my junior year was a big deal.

James was at Morehouse and I was at Clark, so we continued to see each other often. By this time, I had my own car, and I'd even saved up enough money to live off-campus, because living on campus was super expensive. I'd made arrangements to have my second-semester housing expenses paid for, but plans had fallen through.

By that time, James and I were solidly back together, so I asked if I could move in with him and his roommates. It turned out to be the most stressful semester *EVER*!

If I could go back and change some things, I would have never moved in with him. But stupid mistakes mean tremendous triumph after the rain has passed, so I was satisfied with learning from my error.

I guess James again began feeling like he was being crowded— plus, we were young. Therefore other women came into the picture.

Living in a house with a bunch of hormonal, partying college guys was definitely not my idea of romance.

I was so stressed that I knew I had to do something to get myself out of that predicament. I did research online for more scholarships and such, but at first had no luck. I felt alone and afraid. I was upset and always really angry.

I'd pretty much made my mind up—I was never going to suffer and have to depend on someone else for help again. Especially if it meant I had to end up in a sulky living situation.

With little to no moral support at the time, I became a raging beast. I'd stay up all night researching and looking for scholarships and internships I could apply to. This is where my innate "hustle mentality" first spawned.

After the summer came around again, God had blessed me with eleven-thousand dollars in outside funds, and I had landed an internship in DC with a publication company. They contracted me out, and I was even working in my field. I did press releases, traveled to national conferences in New Orleans . . . life was good.

I believed I was done with James. It seemed like the more I took my mind off him, the more life became clear to me and the more successful and hungry for success I became. This was not to say that he was a bad guy. My life's circumstances at the time just called for me to refocus my energy and thoughts someplace else. That was on Monica and her happiness.

James and I continued to remain cordial. He had once again been asked back to New York to intern for a company there. Since I was so close to that city, we spent a few times going back and forth seeing one another. It was great. He was happy and doing well and so was I. After we graduated college, we were still together.

I really believed with all my heart that James would one day marry me. Although I was sure, he seemed so unsure. There continued to be a lot of bickering, and again we broke up.

When I was twenty-five, James and I decided that we'd get back together. He promised me that *NOW* he was ready. A month later, he broke up with me *AGAIN*, for like the millionth time.

I was heartbroken—empty and unsure of why it kept happening.

Of course, there was the problem of not knowing where life was going to lead him and whether I'd fit in. I saw myself as second in importance: I never thought about where life might be leading *me*, and whether *he* would fit in. I believed men were innately more important than women, that their jobs and happiness came before a woman's.

James' philandering continued. Every time another woman walked by, he would allow the brain between his legs to do all the thinking for him. This caused him to constantly question his conflicting desire to remain faithful to one woman.

I cried for days after that last breakup. I didn't know what to do. I called older family members to counsel me. Of course, everyone I spoke with said things like, *Wait for him . . . He seems like he really loves you . . . You've been through a lot. Maybe he's at a rough spot.*

My grandfather would say, "James loves you. Just let time tell. You guys have a great friendship."

Of course, my biological dad was the one to give it to you raw. He said, "Forget that grown boy. You are beautiful, and any guy would be happy to have you. Let that go!"

Listening to my dad sometimes made me angry. I felt if I had grown up with greater examples of how a man should treat a woman, I wouldn't have allowed someone to emotionally abuse me for so long. Who the hell was he to give "love" advice anyway?

I'd begun to realize that I was so much better than what James had to offer. All the pain I'd endured was just not worth it to me anymore. I was empty and incomplete, and so was James.

With all the emotions, stress, and frustration I felt from that relationship, it still couldn't outweigh the fact that I was still in love with him. I just didn't like the fact that I loved him more than he loved me.

Maybe the entire time it wasn't love at all. Maybe it was some false pretense of love. Both of us had some pretty messed-up home situations, so just maybe we meshed so well because we were both screwed and just hungered for some type of affection.

The wise often say that it's completely fine to love someone, but if you can't live with them, then what is the use in continuing?

I'd lost myself in that relationship anyway, and I was completely depleted. I felt as if I had no more love to give. I became very insecure about my appearance, and the confidence that was mostly taken as arrogance was no more.

When I looked into the mirror, I didn't like the Monica I saw. I felt like I wasn't good enough, and I blamed myself often, believing that if my hair were longer, my teeth were straighter, or if I wasn't black, I'd be more appealing.

After I did my time on my job in Atlanta, I had a different perspective on my life. I began to focus on me and my own happiness.

And that's where the idea for my magazine began. I told myself I was free, happy, beautiful, vibrant, and ready to take on the world. I went cold-turkey on James and decided to let years of pain and confusion cease. I packed my bags and got out of Dodge. Everything in Atlanta made me think of him, so I was ready for a fresh start.

3   A Fresh Start

Throwing my bags on the floor, next to the bed in an old and rundown motel room, I knew it was time to get honest. The relationship with James was toxic. It was going to cause me to continue to deplete myself if I didn't get away, and stay away this time. Baltimore, Maryland . . . I'd come here because it seemed like a good, solid city for a new start. A plain, no-nonsense place. A place that I'd never have thought to travel to for pleasure.

I didn't have a lot of money, since I'd just graduated, but it was enough to help me escape the dark and tainted pits of Georgia. I decided that going someplace far and unknown was the best medicine for getting over whatever this sickness was that was plaguing me.

This sickness that I speak of was the illness of internal self-hate. I couldn't stand who I was. When I looked into the broken mirror in the partially lit bathroom, all I saw was someone who didn't amount to anything and must have been a complete waste of time.

I felt broken, used, and like the mere thought of me must have been the most irritating thing a man could ever have on his mind.

I crawled into the back of the bathtub and cried until my vision blurred. I held my head as my birth dad's voice and his nasty language invaded my thoughts.

"You're nothing but a mistake, and I should have flushed your ass down the toilet long ago."

Those words felt like a thousand daggers mutilating me from the inside-out.

How could someone have so much hate for something they created? Kids are supposed to be a blessing, right? Me coming into the world was supposed to be one of the happiest moments of my parents' life.

How could my mother just sit by and allow a man, my own father, to use such destructive words with her gift, her angel in this world—me?

I turned on the water and continued lying in the tub, with all my clothing on. I could see my reflection in the faucet. My eyes were swollen like pillows, and my mascara looked like I'd dressed for Halloween. I took my big toe and played with the faucet stopper until my toes were all wrinkly and the water had lost its warmth.

I retreated to the bedroom and left my wet clothes on the floor. As I crawled into bed naked, I pulled the covers over my shivering body and fluffed a pillow underneath my head. I hadn't eaten all day, but I felt so empty anyway that food wasn't going to fill me. I was yearning for something, and in the dead of night, I knew what it was. I wrapped my arms around myself and hugged myself tightly.

I tilted my head over and kissed my left shoulder, whispering, "I love me, I love me."

When I turned back over, a roach scattered across the dingy walls. I was so lifeless that its mere presence didn't scare me like it normally would have.

As I cut off the light for bed, closing my eyes was as hard as trying to stick two like magnets together. Behind my closed lids, visions of my good times with James played in front of me. Although those moments should have brought a smile to my face, they brought nausea to my stomach and more tears.

I lay in the bed and cried myself to sleep.

The next morning, I stood up, and my entire body felt like I had slammed into a brick wall. When I looked into the mirror, my face looked like chipmunk cheeks. I wet a rag with warm water and patted my eyes until the swelling went down.

After I got dressed, I headed downstairs for breakfast. Given that I was in a new city and in need of a job, I asked the hotel bartender, who looked like she could be my grandmother, for an application.

She asked me what I could do. "I've never seen you around here before. Are you new in town?" she inquired.

"I am. I just graduated with a journalism degree, but I need a job now, so I'll take whatever I can get," I said.

The old woman reached over and pushed my plate to the side. She grabbed my hand and looked me into my eyes.

"I see so much potential in you, but given my many years of wisdom, I see a lot of hurt in you as well. Is there something you'd like to talk about? I'm all ears," she said.

"Well, I just broke up with my boyfriend, and I'm having trouble putting it all back together. It feels like nothing I ever do, when it comes to love, is right. I loved him with every part of me, but . . ."

Before I could finish my last words, I burst into tears. As they dripped down into my orange juice glass, the old woman came around and wrapped her arms tightly around my shoulders.

"It's okay, my dear. I know how this feels. I'm an old woman, and it's happened to me numerous times in my life. I'm seventy-six now. One thing I will tell you is that I'll give you a job here until you get on your feet. I'll also tell you that these feelings are only temporary. I don't know your full story, but what I do know is that God won't put more on you than you can bear. You are worth it, and you are special. Love yourself first, baby! You made the right decision by getting up and walking away from someone who didn't love himself so he didn't know how to love you. Don't allow one fool to ruin it for the rest of the wonderful men that you'll meet in your life. He *IS* out there, believe me. My husband and I have been married for over forty-five years, but before God gave him to me, He tested me and took me through hell and high water until I sat down and listened."

I sniffled, and the old lady handed me a box of Kleenex. "Baby, God is telling you that you need to fix *you* internally. Learn how to love yourself! Take a step back and take responsibility for the part you played, too. We are all flawed. Just remember you are a gift to this world, and you'll one day be a gift to the right man," she said.

I wiped my tears and asked when I could start.

In the next several weeks, the old woman, whose name was Maisy, opened her home up to me and allowed me to rent out a spare room for fifty dollars a month. She said she believed in me and wanted me to save all my money so I could follow my dream and move to New York one day. I told her I was looking to start my own magazine and that I had its layout and design. I just needed the financial power to get it done.

Several months later, I moved out of Maisy's house and into my own place. For the next three-and-a-half years, I lived in Baltimore and worked strategically on my plans for the magazine. I even found a small writing gig that allowed to me to do freelance work when I didn't have to be at the bar.

One day I attended a networking event in town and met a man who would forever change my life. His name was Greg Philips, and he was the owner of one of the elite business magazines in New York. I spewed over with a thirty-second elevator pitch on the dreams for my magazine, and he suddenly was hooked. He genuinely took me under his wing and introduced me to facets of the industry I would have never been able to tap into otherwise.

Months later, he had arranged backers, and I was on my way to New York to launch my magazine. I thanked Maisy for her support and, to this day, I call her weekly because she had made that much of an impact on my life.

Looking back, I didn't regret my decision to dump James once and for all. I didn't even have any ill words on my tongue for him. I merely looked at that aspect of my history as an opportunity to learn and to snatch out the wisdom to apply it to future situations. When I looked in the mirror and my reflection spoke to me, I knew what I had to do. It was time to focus on: being happy. I was done with compromising my self-worth and holding onto relationships that were being built on quicksand. Now that I'd healed, I was ready to hit the dating scene . . . again.

After processing all that had happened to me in recent years, I figured I'd reach out to my home girl Katrina so that we could catch up.

4

I had a date with a big-time sales executive, and I needed to have all of my ducks in a row. I wanted to impress him, but I didn't want him to know I was too interested right away, so I was playing it pretty cool.

I knew if I came across as stand-offish he'd assume I was stuck- up. I knew if I came off too comfortable, he'd think I was easy. This guy would just be another one-night stand to add to the books and make me leave feeling bad about myself.

I'd be headed right back to square one—man-less. I'd have to trash his number after that because every time he'd call, I'd know what it was for: "the booty call."

I wasn't a basic chick, so I demanded and wanted respect. But from those to whom much has been given, much is required, right? I mean, even if this guy wasn't the one, we all need a little R & R, a rebound—a stepping stone, in order to proceed to the next level.

Remember Monica, you are looking for a husband, not a plaything. That's what I'd usually have to say to myself.

Last time I'd been to Atlanta visiting my home girls, they had come up with a method that might help me find a good man. So many crazy ideas had come to mind. There was joining a free relationship site, speed dating, and even the idea of contacting that Patti lady from the matchmaker show.

My mind was boggled, so we decided to link up. We all met at my favorite spot, The Strip, in Atlantic Station, and ordered a few drinks. I thought their idea was silly, but slowly began to consider it after it was thoroughly explained. Clearly, the dating methods I'd been using weren't getting me anywhere.

Katrina, Stephanie, and Ashley all believed they knew what I needed. They suggested that I put my writing skills to the test. This was like the ultimate test! Monica's book of love . . . let it speak for me. They wanted me to keep a journal about my dating experiences.

I'd always used writing as an outlet to describe how I was feeling, but I never really thought about incorporating it into the relationship aspect of my life. For the most part, the situations I journaled about were very personal to me. I didn't share them with others. I felt it would only make me seem weak and vulnerable.

My home girls were somehow convinced that since writing had been a cathartic outlet for my past issues, maybe it would work for my love life as well. I agreed and figured I'd give it a try. After too many drinks and way too much sushi, the plan was forced into action.

Now tonight I had a date with Anthony, and I was expected to take mental notes the entire time, then afterwards write about what I'd gained from my so called dating experience. Until then, I needed to make it home from work, decide what I was going to wear, and call Katrina before my date arrived at 8:30. I had little time to waste.

Finally, after working late, I was off the clock—and stuck in traffic. And on the one day I had a date! Terrific! People in New York can't friggin' drive.

Finally, I made it home and called Katrina.

"Hey, Katrina. What's up, girl?" I said when she answered.

"Nothing much. Just sitting here cooking dinner and listening to Pandora."

At that moment, I knew she must be in one of her moods. That was the only time she cooked and listened to Pandora. Who does that?

"Hey, Katrina, we need to talk about this date. Girl, I'm a nervous wreck. Don't know what I'm gonna wear, and Anthony will be here in less than an hour."

Help! I cried mentally.

Katrina sighed. "Girl, you will be fine. You've got that natural beauty going on, so I'm sure there's not too much dressing you need to do. Just make sure you put on something sexy, but not too sexy. Girl, these guys are a trip. He'll be sitting at the dinner table undressing you with his eyes anyway," she laughed.

After I thought about it, I realized she was right. If I ever wanted to find a man, I needed to relax and have enough confidence to know that the date was going to go well.

"Okay. Well, I'll have to let you go because I need to get ready, but best believe I'll tell you all the details later," I said.

After we hung up, I began to scavenger through my closet looking for something nice to put on.

"All of these damn clothes, and I still have absolutely nothing to wear, aaargg-hhhh," I screeched out loud. I wanted to be sexy but not too sexy; but then again I didn't want to be too casual either!

Looking in the mirror at my figure, I could tell I'd look good in a potato sack. My figure wasn't one of my problems.

I kept glancing at the time, noticing it was just passing by and I still wasn't ready. Anthony could be pulling up at any moment, and I was just standing around in my birthday suit.

I was so nervous.

"Huh, now the phone wants to ring," I said.

"Hello?"

"Hey, I was just calling to let you know I'll be there in about twenty minutes, if that's okay with you," Anthony said.

OMYGOSH. I melted at the sound of his voice. It was deep but not too deep, and I could definitely picture his smile. As I sunk into my couch, I reached over to grab my shirt.

"Okay," I said, and in a moment, we hung up.

I knew good and well I was nowhere near ready to go. "We're going to an Italian restaurant," he had said, so I decided some nicely fitted black pants, pumps, and a loosely fitted shirt would do the trick.

I later added make-up that brought out the colors in my shoes and eyes, without overdoing it, of course—letting the handbag do the rest.

Bam! I was ready. I felt excited and anxious, but a few deep breaths helped me to appear more refreshed.

My hair was bouncing and behaving, and the gym had done my body good. I knew he would be outside in a few minutes, so I had to pull myself together, and I needed to do it quick.

I shook my hands and paced back and forth, trying to think of ways to get rid of my nervousness and sweaty palms, but nothing came to mind.

Then the solution dawned. I would take a shot of tequila and throw some winter-fresh in to kill the alcohol smell. Just one shot to ease the nerves.

At that moment, I ran into the kitchen and took— not one, but two—shots. I knew that by the time we got to the restaurant, I would be good and calm—straight ready for action.

The doorbell rang.

"Oh my gosh, he's here," I muttered.

Trying hard not to get to the door too quickly, I almost slipped and fell. I felt around the room making sure I wasn't leaving anything behind that I'd desperately need later.

Ah-ha! I found my favorite fragrance! J'adore Dior . . . love it.

I spritzed myself a few times, as the doorbell rang a second time. I knew I needed to hurry, because by the third ring . . .

I swung open the door. Anthony stood there.

"Hey. You look very nice," he said.

I froze for a split second and drooled over his beautiful physique and smile. If anything about a man was going to make me melt, it was sure going to be that smile.

"Thank you," I said.

"Ready to go?"

"Yes."

As we began to walk to the car, I saw it. A Maserati! A Gran Turismo, to be exact. I tried my hardest not to seem impressed, because I knew most guys use their sports cars as bait to lure in attractive women.

No, not me, I was different. I was never raised to chase after a man because of his material possessions. Besides, I possessed my own. I had a Jaguar Coupe F-Type sitting covered in the garage.

Hell, it probably isn't even his, I reminded myself. Maybe a rental.

I didn't want to think the worst of Anthony, being that this was our first date, so I loosened up and cut him some slack. The tequila had clearly begun to kick in, and I was feeling better, so I began to talk.

"So, Anthony, how was your day?" I asked.

I didn't even know if that was a good question, but hey, someone had to break the ice.

"Oh, it was good. I actually had to meet with some of my clients, which is why I was running a little late. Sales are a very strategic thing, and you have to bring your 'A' game at all times. That includes putting in some late hours," he said. "What about you?"

I was so busy looking at the seductive movement of his lips that I had missed half of what he said.

"It was great. You know . . . the usual suspects. We're due to release the next issue of my magazine at the end of the month, so it's been deadline after deadline," I said.

I could only hope that my spill was good enough for him to know that I was a really smart woman. But some guys got intimidated by a date who might be more successful than they are, so I mostly focused on him. That wasn't hard to do—Anthony was perfect!

This guy just seemed to have it all—I mean, all I would want and need in a man. He'd gone to the top schools, he was successful, and the cherry on top was that he was fine! How did I come across a man like this?

Then I started to worry that he was too perfect. I am a woman of astute observation, and I tend to go with my first impressions.

We finally arrived. Everything looked amazing. The valet guy opened my door and helped me out. Anthony trotted around to my side of the car and reached for my arm.

"So you're escorting a lady to dinner?" I asked.

I was very nervous but confident. I was only hoping that my make-up hadn't sweated off because the alcohol had me feeling just a little warm.

We began to walk to the restaurant door, and Anthony once again gloated over how beautiful I was. It was a nice gesture, but I don't do too well with overkill.

As we stepped inside the restaurant's doors, a waitress asked Anthony if he had a reservation. I began to feel uncomfortable because he'd all of a sudden recognized the lady that was getting ready to seat us. She was quite attractive, maybe someone he could have been seeing in the past, or maybe I was just looking too deeply into things.

I took a deep breath and stuck my hand out to introduce myself. She gave me a conniving look, but I didn't give a damn. I wanted this heifer to know that Anthony was all mine, even if it was only for one night.

The waitress led us to the table, and Anthony pulled out my chair for me.

I still had spurts of thoughts about why Anthony knew the waitress, but it was only my insecurities stepping in, going for the kill.

Control your thoughts, Monica. Control your thoughts, I told myself. Instead, I excused myself from the table and scurried to the restroom. As I entered, I made sure no one was there and locked the door behind.

I grabbed a wet paper towel, patted my face down, and took a few deep breaths—inhaling and exhaling as my palms lay comfortably on the beautiful marble counter. I naturally assumed dating again wasn't going to be easy, but I had to at least learn to trust the guy a little.

Monica, all guys aren't the same, I told myself.

I began to smile at the beautiful me I saw in the mirror. That caused me snap back to reality. Had I lost track of time? I hurried back to the table.

"Are you okay?" he said as I sat down again. "I thought I was going to have to come in there after you for a second there."

I began to wonder if he had noticed the friction between me and the waitress. Why else would he be asking if I was okay?

"I'm fine. I just needed to wash my hands," I replied.

Anthony quickly changed the subject, and we begin to order.

"I'll have a glass of the Toscana and a house salad," he said.

Hmm, I could see he had good taste in wine.

I ordered the lasagna. I never ordered anything on a date that would be too hard to eat. That would be too embarrassing. Especially with this being our first date. But even the lasagna made me nervous. The last thing I needed was to have sauce all over my face—or worse, a sun-dried tomato stuck between my front teeth.

We patiently waited for the food to be brought out, as an awkward and boring silence lingered over our table. By now my tequila shots had worn off, so I was back to square one of nervousness and sweaty palms.

I envisioned myself in the restroom saying, *You are beautiful, and you can do this.* I began to speak.

"So, what do you like to do when you're not being the big-time sales executive I know you to be? I mean, there has to be something else daunting and interesting about you," I said.

Anthony sighed like he'd had a long day at the office.

"Well, I love camping, believe it or not. I love to get away. Most of the time, I'm stuck in an office negotiating deals or trying to be the big-time sales executive you know me to be," he said with a chuckle.

"Camping gives me a sense of freedom. I can rent a nice quiet cabin in the mountains and just reflect on my life and all that I've accomplished. Late nights by the fire are the icing on the cake."

Ugh, he was amazing. I couldn't believe it, just brilliantly perfect and delicious.

"It's funny that you say that, because as a teen that's all I did," I replied. "I was a complete camp junky. I mean, the downright dirty! We did the hiking, canoeing, caving . . . it was amazing. When I got to college, I sort of got tired of the same ole' and gave it all up. I still love it, though! I have so many memories from those times. My icing on the cake was lying out at night, ten-thousand feet elevation in the mountains, feeling like I could reach up and grab the stars."

Anthony gazed over at me with a look of lust in his eyes. This man was literally hanging on my every word. At that point I didn't know if having his full attention was a good or bad thing.

"You know, Monica, I'm impressed. I would have never taken you for the type to camp. You should come with me sometime. I have a cabin up in Colorado, and it's absolutely beautiful. Very quaint and quiet. I'm sure you'd love it."

"That sounds great," I said, "but maybe we should go on a few more dates before we start our traveling escapades."

"Well, no. I didn't mean to come off too forward, but I'm just a very aggressive man. I see a lot that I like in you. You have a great personality, and it's wonderful to connect with someone that you have 'likes' with," he said, with that charming smile.

I knew he wasn't talking about running off to Colorado right now, but I got scared and guarded when any guy moved to fast. I mean, this could have just been some game for him to juice me up enough to go to bed with him. We all know what they do—men, I mean … make these false promises that are sure to be broken once they got the cookie.

And what about what happens in the horror films?

But women are guilty of the game-playing, too. The world of love is cruel. Maybe love doesn't even exist. I just knew I liked the special feeling it gave me, whatever it was—love?

People are bat-shit crazy—they come off all nice and well-put-together at first, but once they got you, they're sure to show you a side of them you never thought you'd see, so of course I was skeptical about traveling to some deep and dark wooded area with a complete stranger.

"Sure, I didn't mean it like that. I was just joking," I said. We laughed it off, just trying to make light of the situation.

Finally our food arrived, and my stomach was performing a happy dance. I remembered I hadn't eaten anything since earlier in the day.

"Wow, this looks great," I said—when my food was already half-gone.

"I know we should taste each other's. Well, we'll taste whatever you've got left. Gosh, woman, where does it all go?" Anthony joked.

"Sure, and I guess with my rigorous working out, I burn a lot of calories, so by dinner time I'm usually starved," I countered.

At that moment Anthony reached for his extra fork and began to push some of his pasta onto it.

"Open up," he said.

I nervously leaned forward as he gently placed the fork into my mouth. For some strange reason, I closed my eyes too. My taste buds were dancing like crazy; his food was so good.

"Oh my goodness, that has to be some of the best pasta I've tasted in a while," I said.

"Well, I love Italian food, and I come here often, so I'm pretty sure they know just how to prepare it," Anthony said.

Once again, those negative thoughts began to flag in my head. You could go someplace to get lunch or dinner alone, but who the hell does that? I began to think I was really going to have to keep my guard up with this guy.

"Oh, that's interesting. Do you cook?" I asked. "I mean, what are your kitchen skills looking like?"

"Well, I won't say I'm the best, but I can do a lil' somethin'-somethin'," he smiled.

I knew it! I knew he was going to say that he could cook. He was just too perfect; I knew it from the start. I kept swinging back and forth between doubting him and thinking he was perfect.

"Well, who's your inspiration? Did you learn from your grandmother or mom? I love to cook, so I need to see if I got some competition," I said.

"Really!? So it's like that," he said.

"Oh, yeah. It's like that."

Anthony grabbed his napkin, wiped his lips, and sat up straight. I guess he really thought he was going to tell me something.

"My grandmother was a great cook. I spent a lot of my time over at her place as a child, and she taught me a lot. She was very diverse in her cooking, too, so it was always fun to eat. She was the type to surf the Internet just looking for new ideas to bring to the kitchen. I guess that's what spawned my love for cooking," he said. "After she passed a year ago, I pretty much stuck to it. I cook a lot actually—more now than I ever did before."

"I'm sorry to hear about your grandmother's passing. Were you all close?" I asked.

I could see at that point he was vulnerable. Speaking of his grandmother seemed to bring out a softer side of him that most men don't usually like to show. I placed my hand on top of his to console him, and smiled uncomfortably.

"We were fairly close. I mean, she taught me half the little things most women know—sewing my own buttons back on . . . She supported me when I'd left and gone off to the military for a while . . ."

He cleared his throat. "Well, maybe I should get the check. It's getting a little late, and I have a meeting in the morning."

I knew at that moment, a nerve must have been struck. He looked very uneasy and didn't seem to be as excited as he was before. I had to do something! I couldn't possibly let the night end like this.

"I think we should get some dessert before we leave," I said. "I mean, I know it's getting late and you have a meeting in the morning. Believe me, I'm like a zombie when it comes to my work. A lot of late hours and early mornings, but twenty more minutes won't hurt. Come on," I said, batting my eyelashes and giving him what I hoped was a cute smile.

He looked at me with squinted eyes and gave into my idea.

"Okay, why not. I guess that'll cheer me up. Since you looked at me all bushy-tailed and bright-eyed, I can't turn down spending another moment with you," he said.

"I hope I didn't upset you by asking so many questions about your grandmother."

"No, it's completely fine. Don't be silly. It's just a little hard to speak of. She hasn't been gone for that long, so I'm still pretty much coping with it all."

"Well, let's get the waitress and get that dessert," I said.

Anthony had opened my eyes to a new adventure. I was happy with getting to know him. He was sweet, entertaining, and he had a heart.

I guess the scariest thing about getting out there and dating again is that you have to learn all about someone. A complete stranger. You don't know who they are or what they are capable of—for crying out loud, you're literally taking applications for a new best friend! Even a possible life partner.

Shortly after, the waitress arrived, and we ordered the biggest brownie ever. It also had a scoop of vanilla ice cream on top. All I could envision was me waking up with my stomach hanging over the top of my pants.

"I wonder what type of vanilla ice cream this is," I said.

"That's pretty random. What's so good about the 'type' of vanilla ice cream? It's all the same, isn't it?" Anthony asked with a look of interest.

"No, not really. Some are richer than others. I like rich-tasting ice cream. Bluebell is the best vanilla ice cream I've *EVER* tasted. Oh my gosh, if you ever go to any of the southern states you'll have to try it," I said.

Anthony appeared impressed. "I'll have to do that. Why can I only get it in the southern states?"

"Well, that's where it's made. I forgot which state it originates from, but I know that they only sell it in the sixteen southern states."

The waitress once again approached our table. "Are you guys doing okay? Is there anything else you need tonight?"

I looked away.

"No, I think you can just bring us the check," said Anthony. "We're going to head out of here in a sec."

As the waitress walked away, I could have sworn Anthony was looking at her ass! How disrespectful, I mean with me sitting right there!

"Yoo-hoo, over here!" I thought, rolling my eyes in the process.

The waitress returned and attempted to place the check on our table, but it fell to the floor. She bent her voluptuous waist, in what appeared to me a deliberate effort to show off her behind.

All the while, I wanted to become less than a child of God and give her what was on my heart. Instead, I kept it classy, standing up from the table and ignoring her ass, and we proceeded to the front counter to pay.

Anthony opened the door for me and signaled the valet to bring his car. I was exhausted, and I wasn't going to allow some small incident ruin the rest of my night.

I felt sleepy during the ride home. "I had a really great time," I said.

"I did too. We should definitely do this again sometime."

I didn't know if I should respond with a yes, or just wait until he walked me to my door to give a reply. I mean, he was sweet and all. There just seemed to be something about him lurking under the surface.

I couldn't grasp it, but I knew it was something. Or maybe I was doing what most women do: pre-judging the guy before I even really got to know him.

But, come on—the way he'd interacted with the waitress and talked about that restaurant like he'd gone there frequently, probably with other women. Or maybe he was there for innocent business gatherings?

This guy was throwing me for a loop. I didn't know what to think. I just really couldn't fathom him.

"Yeah, we can definitely talk about going out again," I said.

He gave me a blank stare.

"'Yes' would have been a better answer," he said. "Didn't you enjoy yourself?"

"I had a wonderful time. I'll call you this weekend, and we'll go from there?"

Anthony didn't look too happy about my response, but had no choice but to respect it. He gazed over at me and then back at the road.

"Okay. I'll take that," he smiled.

We soon arrived at the doorstep of my exquisite bachelorette pad. I knew that the night would either end with a kiss or a hug . . . hmmm.

It was lame, but I'd once read an article that said if you hugged someone, you should hug for at least twenty seconds to feel the full "love" effect. I was nervous— that was long-ass time! How a person could hug someone for that long without it feeling awkward, was beyond me.

My thoughts began to fade. I figured it would be nice just to clear my mind for once and go with the damn flow. We women do too much sometimes. That includes but is not limited to overthinking everything.

I smiled and waited for Anthony to come around and open my door. I had to give it to the man, he was quite the gentleman. I couldn't remember the last time I'd gone on a date and the guy did the old-fashioned door-opening tricks.

I slowly got out of the car as Anthony gazed at me.

"So, I guess this is the end?" he said sarcastically.

"Well, it doesn't have to necessarily be the end, unless you really want it to be," I smiled.

"I just want you to know that I had a great time, and I'll definitely be waiting for your call. I'm looking forward to us going out again," he said, in a serious voice.

At that moment he went in for the kill . . . a hug. I awkwardly stood there—my arms embracing him, pouched lips. He hugged me almost like he never wanted to let go. It was electric, warm, and soft. We hugged for a while, and after a bit, it no longer felt awkward.

As we parted from the hug, he gazed into my eyes and landed a passionate kiss on my lips. My lip gloss was poppin', so when he pulled away, it felt like he was peeling a sticker from an apple.

Slow, sensual, and seductive. My toes tingled a little, and my heart was in my throat.

Anthony went in for another kiss, but this one was deeper.

It felt like the sun had suddenly appeared, beaming its hot rays of warmth right down on us. Anthony cocked his head to the right, and he interlocked his tongue with mine, circling it over and over again in a slow figure-eight motion. As I attempted to pull away, he moved his hands down to the small of my back and pulled me in tighter. His teeth gripped my bottom lip. When he finally let go, the tip of his tongue stroked the bottom of my lips up to the tip of my nose.

"You have a good night, okay?" he said.

"You too," I said, feeling weak in the legs.

This guy literally walked away like he hadn't just made love to my mouth.

As he drove off, my body stood still, twitching like it was about to have a seizure. I pulled my handbag up and breathed in and out. The man had left me turned on like a fire hydrant.

I walked into my bedroom and grabbed a notebook, just thinking about the deal I'd made with my girls. I was supposed to go on dates and use my poetry and writing expertise to describe what I was feeling about each potential life partner . . . husband . . . I guessed that was a good thing. It was definitely an excellent tool for filtering out the men that just weren't even worth the time.

I didn't even know where I'd start with this man. I knew he was smart and sexy, but he seemed to have another side, something underlying and mysterious . . . maybe. I was such an emotional person that it always got to me when I couldn't read someone the way I wanted to read them.

I guess I'd describe Anthony as a free spirit, someone who didn't seem to have cares because he was successful. Yet he was mysterious and sexy. For godsakes, I'd already pre-judged the man by the way he was interacting with a waitress!

He'd made up for it, though, by sexually inciting my lips when he brought me home.

I started to think that Anthony would be a man who would drive me insane . . . in a good or bad way. He seemed to have the juice to keep me mentally satisfied, and he was able to break down every itching sexual wall with just a kiss— however, he had roving eyes and had given me feelings of mistrust.

So I put pen to paper:

Midnight Dreams

I dreamed of a love like you

Wishing, hoping, and praying that one day my dream would come true

Looking to the stars before falling asleep

Holding a picture close to my heart was more than I could keep

When I go to sleep tonight, I don't really know what I'll dream of next

Maybe a shooting star to make a wish upon would be best

I don't really know what dreams may come. . .

About in my life

Pushing through tough times, hell and strife

I continue to look for love in all the wrong places

Always searching for new spaces

Then at the end, another's heart is left broken

Words left lingering and unspoken

At one point and time, I knew I had a true love

But what is love?

I've made mistakes that I really can't fix

And now I realize it's him that I miss

Cheered me up and always made me laugh

Gave me things I always wanted to have . . .

Love for someone and the all-above trust;

But now he's messed it all up so his face I no longer touch

Day by day we drift further away from each other

I know he's probably found another . . .

Person— love—who has what I don't

Looks, obsession . . . things that I want . . .

I guess all I can do now, is think of what I may dream of tonight

A love that I mistook in all the wrong sights

I would apologize if I didn't get around him and melt

Looking into his eyes and feeling things I've never felt and only dreamt

I want to open up and express myself but something always holds me back

It's frustration and nervousness that I NEVER lack.

Ugh! What was wrong with me! My mind was all over the place. I wanted to call Katrina, but didn't want to get her out of bed. I wanted to tell her how amazing this guy was. Could this be too good to be true? Had I found what I was looking for all this time? Or just like in the poem, was there a secretive side about him that I hadn't seen or discovered yet?

Mixed Messages

5

Do you believe in love, in love, in real love . . . good love? Casey Johnson was playing in the background the next morning, as I sulked. The date had gone well, but I was uneasy. The entire time we had been at dinner, I had let my insecurities rule my universe. I kept thinking about Anthony staring at the waitress, and him visiting the restaurant too often. What the hell was wrong with me?

I grabbed the phone to call Katrina. She answered on the first ring, and for a moment, I hesitated.

"Hello? Monica, you there?"

"Yes, girl. I have *WAY* too much to tell you."

In an instant, I drifted back to how wonderful this man was—could be, if I just allowed myself to relax and go with the flow. You know, if I could just chill for a minute.

"So what happened? Did you have fun, and how did he look? Was he dressed nice? I know you hugged him at the end of the date. What did he smell like?" she asked, full of excitement.

Katrina could be so thirsty. I mean, asking me all those questions?

"Next time I see you, I'll have a Sprite for you. You need to quench all the thirst you're having right now, waiting to hear about this guy. Okay, be juiced up all you want, because, girl, he was so fine," I said.

"Shut up! Tell me more," she said.

"I can't even describe him all in one word. You would have had to be cupid on my shoulder to experience what I felt when he first picked me up. I mean his whole swag was on point."

"Well, what did he think of you?" she asked.

"He thought I was beautiful, but you know what? That's not even the real reason I called, so I'm going to stop fronting," I said.

I realized I had to tell Katrina the full story, or else this whole project was doomed. I mean, unless I wanted to be lonely forever, it was time to fess up.

"Okay, so the date was nice and all, but I started acting stale." I said.

"What do you mean by that? Now Monica, you've worked too hard to mess stuff up now. Ya'll have only been on one date. You're going to run the guy off before he even gets a real chance to know you. Every guy is not like your father. You're the one that's always grilling me about controlling my thoughts! Look at you not taking your own advice," she said.

"Come on, Katrina, this is stuff I already know. I'm sure I don't need to take this advice off of someone who has already had a failed marriage!" I snapped.

At that moment, I knew I'd hit a nerve. That was a really low blow! Katrina was sure to *NEVER* talk to me again after that.

"Now Monica, you know that wasn't right. You lucky we be girls for a minute, otherwise I would hang up on your ass. Look, I know you're frustrated, but this is only the beginning to a very beautiful journey, if you allow it," she said. "Yes, I was married and divorced once, but that taught me a lesson. I was working against God, and that's not what He had in store for me. Now I have Tyrell, and he is one of the best things that's ever happened to me in my life. I can't stress that enough."

She reacted in a way that was completely unexpected. I thought she was fixing to let me have it for sure!

"Well, I do apologize, and that was a very low blow. We are way too grown for all that! I definitely feel what you're saying, it's just so hard. Hell, if I never marry and have kids, I'm going to continue to save up and travel the world," I said.

"Don't say that, girl. Everything happens for a reason. Your book of life is already complete. What is for you *WILL BE* for you," she said.

"One last question, did he kiss you?" she asked.

"Yes, girl, he kissed me. And let me tell you, it left me pretty turned on!" I said.

Restless from the night, I just wanted to end my conversation with Katrina. Even though she'd given me some really great advice, I didn't want to talk more about the date yet.

"Hey girl, I have to go. Got a meeting this the morning and a deadline for the next issue. We'll definitely be talking more about this soon," I said. "Thanks for all that lovely advice. Now I can breathe again," I added.

"Okay. Well, I accept your apology, but just remain patient. We all know that your ass is getting old and that clock is ticking. But you wait and see what God is going to bless you with. Well, head on out to work now."

"You always know what to say to make a girl feel better."

"Well, that's what I'm here for," she answered.

After hanging up, I grabbed my notebook and clenched it close.

Having faith and writing in that thing was a definite release strategy for me. I'd written for work and stuff, but that was all just to pay the bills. Writing poems and my own personal thoughts and feelings was freeing. I could keep them to myself, or share if I so chose. There was no judgment behind my words, because they were private. I was free to self-express.

My pages didn't talk back or judge, and they'd even caught my tears every so often. That journal of mine was my heart.

The next morning at work, things were so crazy. People were running around like little chickens with their heads cut off, trying to get pieces to my desk for final review. Pictures had to be photo-shopped and every mistake had to be corrected. I had exactly a week to get this damn magazine to print.

"Good morning," Blake said sluggishly.

Blake worked in the advertising department. I loved him dearly, but wasn't expecting to see him in my office this early. *UGH!*

As usual, I put on my little fake little smile and proceeded to ask him what the heck he wanted so early in the morning.

"I'm all good, but we have a little problem," he said through clenched teeth.

"What seems to be the issue?"

The way this man looked was pathetic. How could it be *that* bad? No, it *couldn't* be that bad, because the magazine was going to print next week whether we liked it or not. At that moment, I held my frustration and calmly said what I needed to say.

"Okay, Blake, I'm very busy. The magazine is going to print next week. My phones will be ringing off the hook in a few minutes, and I have a million documents to look over by day's end. Hell, I'll probably be here until the wee hours of the morning. *SO*, here is what I want you to do," I said.

Blake stared at me.

"I want you to fix it," I said.

"Fix it?"

"Yes! Fix it. I trust your judgment. I mean, I made you the manager of the ad department for a reason, didn't I?" I asked.

Blake scurried out of my office, and I ran for a cup of coffee. I just knew it would be a long day and long night.

After leaving the office at about four in the morning. I was beat. I had about thirty missed calls, a hundred text messages, and a hundred more voicemails to check. The next issue was essentially ready to go to press, and I felt complete. We still needed a few photos, but Blake was going to take care of that, so we were good. Whatever his problem was from the morning, it seemed he had resolved it.

As I stepped inside the door of my house, the sun was rising and the phone was ringing. *AHHHH!* It was Anthony.

"But why so early in the morning?" I thought.

Even though I wanted to answer, I didn't. I mean, who called someone at 4:30 a.m.? I decided to let him leave a voicemail, as I retreated to the shower to wash away all the previous day's stress.

A few hours later, I rose to the sound of an annoying alarm clock. Ugh, another day.

I felt so drained, but I needed to work out. It was the only thing that would keep my body banging. I walked into the kitchen to make coffee and a piece of toast.

At that moment, I noticed a few missed calls followed by voicemails. I clicked on "play."

"Hey, this is Anthony. I know it's late, but I was wondering if I could see you. I know you work late nights, so I assumed you'd be up. Call me as soon as you get this."

"Oh, hell no!" I yelled.

At that moment, I picked up the phone and called Katrina, waking her up super early like I had some heartbreaking news.

As the phone rang, I felt irritated. I felt like a piece of meat, just waiting to be fed to another lion.

What if this "lover boy" was just another player?

"Hello," Katrina answered, sounding like a seventy-year-old man with a throat infection.

"Hey girl. I know it's really early, but you are not going to believe this shit," I said.

I could hear Katrina wrestling to get out of bed. I knew she was thirsty for a good story; that was just the way she rolled.

"Naw, you good, girl. I need to get up anyway. So what happened? Is it about Anthony?"

I really wanted to tell Katrina what a jerk Anthony had turned out to be, but I liked him too much.

"Anthony decided to call me at like 4:30 this morning. I started to answer the phone, but I didn't after I realized how late it was. He said he wanted to see me. I had literally just walked in from the office," I said.

Katrina sat silent for a moment, but I knew she was ready to explode with advice.

"Girl, that ain't nothing. First off, what did the voicemail say? I mean you can't just go jumping to conclusions," she said annoyingly.

This heifa is crazy. Did she really just tell me not to trip?

"What do you mean? Did you hear me say what time it was?" I asked.

"I wasn't saying it like that. You have to look at every situation with two lenses, girl. I keep telling you that *ALL* guys aren't the same. You said you guys had spoken about your late nights before. He didn't say he wanted to see you at four-thirty in the morning—maybe he wanted to do a mid-day lunch or something. But like I said, *HE DIDN'T* say, so you shouldn't be so ready and willing to write him off so soon. See, that's why your ass is still single now," she laughed.

Katrina did make a good point, but by the same token, I wasn't sure if I was ready to go all in. I knew I shouldn't go into situations ready to give up too soon, but this one may have been too hard to mend.

When you're thirty, you don't have time for games. Most people would also say that when you're thirty, you have really become a woman. You are confident in yourself and true to your words and aspirations. I was honestly starting to feel like I was thirty, but I still had a few insecurities that needed to be tamed. I was a *little* insecure but hungry for whatever I was supposed to have next.

"I see what you're saying, girl," I said, "but you already know how I am. Maybe I'll give him a call this eve to see what that was all about."

"Okay, but don't do it with an attitude!" Katrina said.

As we hung up the phone, I just kept having second thoughts about still kicking it with Anthony. At the end of the day, I could seek advice from Jesus, and the decision would still be completely up to me.

I headed to the gym with a clouded mind. I got on the treadmill and ran for about thirty minutes—just enough to break a sweat. As I headed back to my place, my cell phone rang. It was him.

"Hello," I said.

"Hey, I know I called you earlier this morning, I hope you didn't take it the wrong way."

As those words rolled off of his tongue and into my ears, I knew he'd be trying to cover his tracks. So I lied.

"No, I was up anyway. I'd stepped in the shower and when I got out, I hit the sack. I had a *VERY* long and drawn-out day," I said.

"Okay. Well, that's quite understandable. I didn't want to come on too strong, but I really enjoyed our date the other night. I feel like we had a very strong connection. So, with that said, I was wondering if you'd like to have lunch with me today."

Katrina was right. He just wanted to ask me out to lunch. So since he was so persistent, I decided to give him one more shot.

"Okay, that sounds good. I was going to leave the office early anyway to catch up on some much-needed rest," I said.

"I know all about that! Since you're tired, I won't hold you hostage for too long. Let's say we meet at the little pizza spot right on the corner of 113th Street," he said.

At that moment, I figured he was trying to reel me back in.

He'd completely twisted things with calling me at 4:30 a.m.—like, how do you even make that sound good?

Hanging up my phone, I reached for something comfy to wear to work. Since it was going to be a short day for me and a pizza lunch, I figured I didn't need to be too snazzy.

As I went through the morning, time kind of stood still. I didn't have much work to do, and my body and mind fluttered with all types of thoughts and emotions. I reached into my purse and grabbed my notebook. Everyone was working, and my phone hadn't rung in hours, so I began to write.

Just as my pen got ready to touch paper, my cell rang. It was from a number I didn't recognize. I assumed it could be important, so I answered.

"Hello, who am I speaking with?" I asked.

"This is Jerome," the voice on the other end said.

As his deep, sexy voice quivered through the phone, I knew exactly who he was.

Jerome had been my Atlanta beau, during times when James and I were broken up. We never really got serious because he didn't have too much going for himself. The only thing he did have going was some great sex.

"I was just hitting you because I'm in your town. Was wondering if we could meet," he said.

"Um, I'm not sure because I have a few things to do today. Depends on what time. How long are you here for?" I asked.

"Until tomorrow night. I just came out here to see one of my little shorties."

I knew exactly what he was referring to: one of his little girls.

Jerome had three different babies by three different women. That was another reason we couldn't ever be down because he was the king of raw dogging, and I wasn't for all the baby mama drama.

"Well, okay," I said. "We could meet tonight sometime if you want."

He didn't know, but the reason I wanted to see him was he had exactly the moves I was hungering for, after a long dry spell.

Humph, I thought to myself. *I better go get some condoms because I don't know what this guy's been doing.*

"You give me a time and place," he said. "I'll be there."

Hanging up the phone, I smiled slyly. Clenching my notebook, I remembered I was supposed to be journaling and finding a good relationship, not making sex dates! I picked up my pen and began to write:

Who are you to me?

I don't trust you, I don't love you, so what is this supposed to be?

Lust . . . laughs . . . and continuous pain.

I'm trying my BEST to not believe that all men are the same.

But this guy is manipulating my soul, my mind.

Please God, don't tell me I'm just knocking off more precious time

Searching, digging, and delving for the right one.

Jerome had given me the inspiration I needed to spit out a few poetic lines.

As I started to put my journal back in my purse, I noticed the time. It was almost ten after twelve, and I still hadn't left the office. I decided that taking the train would be faster than driving in the hectic city traffic. The streets of New York were way too crazy during the lunch hour.

When I arrived at the pizza spot, Anthony was already there. He tossed me a look of suspicion, but I wasn't quite sure what that was all about. He was gazing over the restaurant like he was watching his back or something.

"Hey!" I called from across the room.

We scrambled through lunch traffic to reach each other, and he wrapped his arms around me. I closed my eyes and melted, almost like I did on our first date. He smelled so fresh and clean. When I looked up, his gorgeous smile was lighting up the room.

"You ready to order?" he asked.

I was so busy undressing him with my eyes that I didn't register his question.

"Hey, daydreamer. You ready to order?" he repeated.

"Oh, yeah. I was just thinking about all the stuff I have to take care of when I get home," I lied.

As Anthony ordered our pizza, I scoped the room for a place to sit. The place was way too packed.

"Hey, Anthony, there's a seat by the window," I said.

As we headed for the table, another couple sat down in our spot.

"Darn! That was the last open table," I shouted. The room was so loud it crowded, it felt like a circus.

"That's okay. We can go for a walk," he said. "The best way to eat New York-style pizza is on the go."

As we left, he wrapped one hand around my waist. I wasn't expecting it, so I clumsily tripped out the door and fell flat on my butt, dropping my pizza as I went down.

"I am so sorry!" Anthony let out a loud and obnoxious giggle.

I was so embarrassed! Everyone was looking, and random people walking past were trying to help me up.

" I'm fine, thanks," I told them, giggling, too.

"Well, there goes your lunch," Anthony said.

"I'm such a klutz. That line is way too long, and I have to be back to the office in thirty minutes since I'm leaving early today."

"Well, that's okay. Since I'm such a gentleman, you can have some of mine," Anthony insisted.

"No. I don't want to eat your lunch," I said.

We began to walk away from the pizza spot.

Anthony reached for a napkin and tore his greasy slice in half so he could give me a piece anyway.

"Aw, thank you. That's so sweet. And look, you even gave me the bigger half," I laughed. "Now there goes all that hard work I put in at the gym this morning."

Anthony waved his hand, I guess to indicate that I was fine.

He then pulled up his sleeve to check the time. "Well, I really enjoyed our mini-date, but I've got to get back to the office, too. Duty calls. There's a meeting soon I can't be late for," he said.

He kissed me on the cheek and tramped toward the nearest train stop.

I reached for my cell to see if there had been any missed calls. There were. Mostly business.

When I returned to the office, I finished my work, then straightened up my desk and got ready to leave. Blake had IM'd me saying he'd have the last pictures for the issue to my email by midnight. As I left the office, he came down the hall toward me.

"Yes, Blake," I said.

"I just wanted to make sure you'd got my IM," he replied, hesitantly.

I never understood why people got so nervous whenever they had to report to the boss. I mean, was I that uptight? Well, I didn't think I was that bad, but I knew my title kept people choking on their drinks.

"Yes, I got it. I'll look for the photos in my email around midnight. And by the way, loosen up a little. No worries. You're doing a great job," I said, slugging him on the shoulder.

Blake scurried away, and I headed for the front door. I had a very interesting night awaiting me.

6   Jerome

When I arrived home, I began sifting through my "sexy" drawer. I figured something black and sleek would do the trick. Hell, it was going to be coming off anyway.

I slipped on some fitted black pants and a loose off-the-shoulder-type shirt and headed to fix dinner. I knew when Jerome arrived he'd want to eat. He loved my shrimp-over-salad and seared steak, so that was on the menu, along with some white wine, of course.

I spruced the place up and set the table with candles. As I plopped down on the couch for a quick nap, the phone rang.

Darn, I can't ever catch a break, I thought.

"Hey, Ma, it's Jerome," I heard when I answered. "I'm just hitting you to let you know I'll be out that way within the next hour. Is that cool?" he asked.

"That's fine. I'll be here," I said.

Hanging up the phone, I kept thinking about how sleep-deprived I was. Since dinner was near ready and the table was set, I put on an alarm for a thirty-minute cat nap.

It felt like I'd just dozed off when the doorbell rang. I knew it was Jerome but didn't expect him to show so soon. I yelled for him to wait a minute. I rushed to the bathroom, rinsed my mouth, brushed my hair, and washed my face. I clumsily hurried to the table and lit the candles. The doorbell rang again.

I opened the door, and Jerome walked in. Just like a thuggish guy.

"Hey, was you sleeping or something? You look mad tired," he said.

"Yeah, I dozed off for a minute. So what's been up with you? I haven't seen you in such a long time. Go ahead and make yourself at home."

I took his coat and noticed he was wearing my favorite scent. If there was anything I could say about my likes in a man, it was that I could way-easy go for a guy who kept himself smelling like a million bucks.

"You look beautiful as always," he smiled.

"Thanks. I just threw some stuff on," I said, fluffing my hair. "I figured since you were coming by, I'd make your favorite dish. We have seared steak and shrimp-over-salad with wine."

Before I could even tell him what was for desert, he swept me off my feet. He began to kiss me like he always had before, and headed for my bed, with me in his arms. He ripped my shirt off as I unbuckled his pants.

"Um, no sir."

"What's wrong, Ma? I was just trying to set the mood," he said.

"I know, and you can set the mood by first putting on a condom. Don't worry. I've got you covered," I said, reaching for the night stand. Condom problem solved.

The love-making was fantastic. My body was feeling things it hadn't felt in months, and I loved every moment of it.

Afterwards, we lay there, breathing heavily. I was satisfied.

The next morning, Jerome showered and headed out. His flight was leaving soon, so he was in a hurry.

"I had a great night, Ma. It's always good to see old and beautiful faces," he smiled.

"Likewise," I said.

As he left, I noticed it was half-past eight, and I had to be at work by ten. What a day it was going to be! It was a Saturday, but the work for an owner is never done. The magazine was dropping Monday at noon, so everything had to be in place by day's end.

The office was quiet because everyone was off except for the main team. The advertising and marketing group was in, along with a few writers who needed to spruce up their articles.

All day at work, I couldn't think about anything but the night with Jerome. Even though he didn't have much else to offer, he sure did know how to satisfy a woman sexually. But although the night was good, I felt down. I mean, the sex was nice, but I wanted to have it all. You know, I wanted a man to come home to me at night, too. Well, I had to forget about it. Jerome could never be anything more than a plaything, and I think he knew it.

Monday came, and the magazine wasn't ready. Everything had to be pushed back several days. I sat at my desk, in the Monday-morning stupor, re-evaluating my decision to sleep with Jerome. I wasn't sure it was my best-ever idea. Sure, it had felt spectacular, but it didn't really fit with my resolve to find Mr. Right, my own true legit man. Maybe I'd kind of cheated myself, going down a side road when what I really wanted could only be reached by staying on the highway.

I decided to call Anthony. It was getting close to lunchtime, and I figured he'd be up for it, even though I had the Monday drags.

I phoned. No answer.

Since Anthony worked near Times Square, which was only a short train ride away, I decided I'd leave, grab lunch for both of us, drop by his office, and surprise him. I stopped at one of the markets when I suddenly heard a voice.

When I got on the train, it was packed. There were way too many people! I was beyond irritated, and still had two more stops to go. You couldn't even scratch an itch if you had one.

I finally arrived at Anthony's stop. *Now to ride the elevator up like a million floors,* I thought.

When I finally got to Anthony's floor, his assistant wasn't there. I walked past her desk and found his door. I knocked. No one answered, so I made the executive decision to barge in.

"What the hell is going on?" I screamed.

There was Anthony, in all his glory, banging some girl on top of what appeared to be his desk.

Her legs were in a v-shaped position, wrapped around his lower back. All I got was a view of the skyline from Anthony's office and his sweaty ass chops.

"Hell, no. I knew something wasn't right about your ass. Remember? The night you bragged about that Italian restaurant and how you always go there?" I yelled.

Anthony was speechless.

"I am so sorry," I said to the girl. "I didn't know he was seeing anyone else." She screeched as she scrambled for her clothes.

"Lady, you don't say anything to me? You're his secretary or something?"

I turned my anger on Anthony. "All that talk about how you were going to treat me right? You'd say anything to get a quick nut. I thought you were a genuine guy, but you know what? You can't be any better than the dirt on the bottom of my shoe. Lose my fucking number, and finish screwing her ass," I yelled.

"And by the way, I brought your trif ass lunch," I said, throwing the bag on the floor.

"Please! Wait! Just let me explain."

"Explain what, Anthony? You ain't nothing but a two-timing loser, and I deserve better. I demand better. We are too grown-up for this. You've lost my trust. Where is the respect? There's nothing left to say. You're not who you say you are. I need some-one legit, honest, and upfront. If you wanted to see other people, you could have told me so. At least have the decency not to bring your side pieces to where business should be taking place. The pain I feel right now makes we want to cry, but you'll never see my vulnerability. Get the hell out of my way."

As I brushed past him and pushed through his front glass doors, other employ-ees stared to get a glimpse of what was going on.

That night, my phone must have rung a million times. I wasn't answering on anyone, not even my home girls. I knew I shouldn't have lost my temper in Anthony's office, but the shock had brought up so much anger and pain from the past. I had just screwed Jerome the night before, but I wasn't feeling too bad about it now, since Anthony was screwing his secretary.

I begin to think about what would have happened if the tables were turned. What if Anthony had walked in on me screwing Jerome? Who would be the one spitting-mad then? I was cursing Anthony for being a two-timing traitor, but hadn't I done the same thing to him the night before? Was I deceiving myself, applying a double standard—it's wrong if you do it, mister, but fine if I do it?

I realized I didn't have the right to be so mad. We'd only been on couple of dates, but I guess we should have communicated about what each person wanted from the start. Who was to blame here?

I began to doze off, and my phone rang again. It was Anthony, of course. I didn't want to talk to him, but I needed to get him off my back, so I answered.

"Anthony, what do you want?" I asked sheepishly.

"Baby, I'm sorry. I mean I wasn't expecting you to just pop up on me like that. Sheila doesn't mean anything to me. I want you," he said.

As the words rolled off his tongue, I made fun of him by mocking his every word with my hands.

"Let me tell you something, Anthony. I've heard it all, okay? This little game that all of you men want to continue to play on us women is running real dry. I don't have time for this! I'm thirty years old, and I'm ready for something substantial, so if you aren't, then you should have said that from the very beginning. That would have kept my feelings from getting hurt, so with that being said, we're through. I already don't trust you, and I definitely won't trust that you'll stop screwing another woman behind my back," I said.

Why was I so upset, though? I had clearly been playing the same game Anthony was playing. Was it a game, or was it just poor decision-making and bad communication skills?

I began to believe that maybe I didn't have it all figured out and maybe I didn't even know what I wanted for myself. Did I honestly and truly want a relationship, and the commitment that required? Or was I just lonely and looking for something easy to fill the void?

Men and women seemed to wake up daily to the fact that they wanted something different. I was living proof of that. Maybe we were both filled with unrealistic expectations from the start.

"Just give me another chance to make it right," he was saying. "Don't you believe in second chances?"

"Yes, I do. But in your case, I don't. You see, all this second-chancing is why I'm still alone, so it was nice knowing you. Goodbye." I hung up the phone.

Anthony called back a second later. I quickly clicked the "ignore" button.

Back to square one for me! I was confused about the reasons for my behavior and what I truly wanted. Was I set on sabotaging myself, on spoiling my chances for happiness? Could I be trusted to be faithful to one man? Was I a legit woman? Or was I a superficial fool, determined to waste my life on superficial hook-ups?

One thing, for sure though, I had learned: the reason why people say "Call before you show up."

On the Road Again

8

The next morning, I rose with words on my heart. I felt like I needed to write to relieve some the stress from the day before. It was now Tuesday, and I had to head to the office because we were days away from release.

With the way Anthony had treated me, I was feeling a little worthless again. I wasn't getting any younger, and neither was my soul or spirit.

He had done the ultimate no-no, so there were no second chances after that, right? I mean who would settle for a guy who clearly only has his mind on one thing: to screw everything that has legs?

To me it was amazing to see how we human beings worked. I'd clearly fooled around with Jerome a few nights before, so why was I so upset that Anthony was screwing his assistant? I mean, two can play that game, right? You reap what you sow. Karma is a bitch.

I guessed if all of us had the screw-around mindset, we'd never get anywhere. Especially we black women and men. Where was the love? Did that even still exist with us? Divorce rates sky-high, and the only thing men had to follow now was cash, clothes, and hoes . . . so why would they want to tie down?

Maybe I was thinking about the situation too much. I was just really beginning to see that the "new love" had been no love at all.

As I collected my thoughts, I sought after ways to get over Anthony. Maybe I'd go shopping, work out . . . you know, make up some type of routine that would involve me. Get my mind off those men for a while.

At that moment, I hit on it: a trip with the girls! Yes! That's what I needed. It was going down! When I say that, I mean it was literally going to go down, as in "somewhere south"—someplace real exotic, where the men would be fine and exotic too.

I pondered about ideas for hotels, sites to see, and foods I wanted to eat. I figured pure excitement and a little discussion with the girls would help us find the right destination.

Since I was so excited now, about taking a trip, thoughts about Jerome and Anthony faded into the background. There were so many other men out there, and looking at who I was, I really didn't need to be sulking over some loser. I decided to write a poem before leaving for work:

Kiss It All Goodbye

You know, you kind of had it made

But since you're so selfish and self-acclaimed

Let all memories of me disappear, let them burn, fade.

I only gave you half of me, and I, you gave half of you.

I never understood it. Why tell someone something if it wasn't true?

You weren't looking for anything substantial, just to have something to own.

You wanna tat yo' name on that,

Get you an easy chick . . . a plaything . . . something to bone.

If I was cupid and you were my arrow, I'd break you in half,

Throw you about like a piece of crap,

Wouldn't feel bad about it—I might just laugh.

From this day forward, you can kiss it all goodbye.

Go live your life the way you want to: self-acclaimed and dry.

If there is anything that can be taken from this,

Lesson learned and lived,

It's that seeing your true colors before I lost my heart was a divine gift.

Ah! I felt so damn good. It felt great to have closed that chapter, and now I was ready for a whole new one, I thought.

What I'd learned from my experience with Anthony was that communication is key. We'd never laid out our expectations from the beginning, and so that left us in limbo. There was this sense of confusion as to what we both may have truly wanted. We'd both engaged in external affairs which caused the demise of our relationship before it even had a chance to start.

Internally, I blamed myself because I set a standard I wanted Anthony to meet but I wasn't meeting it myself. Not only was I not meeting it, but I hadn't even expressed it to Anthony. As a woman, it was my responsibility to respect myself enough not to only practice what I preached but to be brave enough to teach men how I should be treated.

Later that morning, I still had not heard anything back from Blake about the last photos. The magazine was pretty much finished, but we were one day away from going to press. What the heck was he doing?

The entire train ride to work had felt devastating. I had so many feelings going on in my body that it felt like I would explode. Work, love, friends, and even family were starting to cloud my judgment about my true purpose. I really needed to let all of my personal thoughts blow over and concentrate on the magazine dropping.

When I got to the office, things had been loud and chaotic as usual. Chairs were clanging, people were running to get coffee, and my desk was full of documents to look at. *Lord, take me now,* I thought.

Sifting through all the mess, I'd come across a sealed envelope. There was no name on it. As a matter of fact, there was nothing on it at all.

Damn. Is he really that mad at me? I thought. Thinking that Anthony was probably trying to pull some sick and twisted joke, like sending me fake anthrax, I threw the envelope away.

Seconds later, my curiosity got the better of me. I retrieved the sealed envelope from my wastebasket. I opened it, and sure enough, there was a letter from Anthony. Wanting to know what he could possibly have to say, I read:

Hey beautiful

I know that what I did was trashy and completely out of character. I say that it was out of character because I know what type of person I portrayed myself to be to you. Please don't hate me. I'm not perfect, but I know that you are. We could have made something beautiful, and I screwed it up, I'll admit. I'm not writing this just to get back in good with you; I just wanted to genuinely apologize. Take care.

Anthony

Wow. I mean, was he kidding me? Do all guys seriously think they can just apologize and expect the crooked to be straight, all of their wrongs to be turned right?

Anthony was a likable man—a gentlemen even. I knew deep down in my heart that he was someone's man, just not mine. We'd both started off on the wrong foot.

I sat in the office the rest of the morning, mostly daydreaming, not really focused on work. My heart was sunken, and my ego had been bruised. I knew I was a woman of stubborn ways and that this sort of attitude would never be appealing to a man.

I'd come to the conclusion that, in order for me to love any man, I had to learn to love me first. The hardest thing to do for anyone was to learn, let go of old baggage, and be ready to take on something new, with a clean heart. Not be some ole' stomped-on and depressed chic. I knew what I had to do.

The advertising crew and the team that put the magazine together came by to claim all last inputs. I called a meeting to make sure everything was in place. I called Blake into my office.

"Please be sure to add those last photos here and here," I said, indicating the blank slots in the computer layout where the missing pictures should go.

He nodded.

"LETS GO, TEAM," I yelled out to the office.

Everyone began clapping and hooting because our second issue was ready to hit the press. Not only that, but the job was done before noon, so I was free to go.

After leaving the office, I needed something to get my mind off of all of the mishaps that were keeping me from finding a good man. I needed some *ME TIME*! I couldn't wait for that exotic vacation with the home girls I'd been imagining. I needed a pedi and a mani, a little pink moscato, and a good book by the fire.

It all seemed so appealing, but I kept thinking of Anthony. How he'd made me laugh, our interests . . . shit, all of that should have trumped whatever I thought he had going on with that waitress or even his secretary back at his office. Maybe he saw something special in me. Was I making a mistake? Was I being two-faced and stubborn?

The first night we'd gone out, he never once asked to come up for a nightcap like some of the other low-down busters. At that moment, I couldn't tell whether I really wanted Anthony back or if it was all just an excuse I was manufacturing to avoid being alone for the next several weeks.

I had gone to church the previous Sunday. It was almost like the pastor had been an angel on my shoulder all week long. He'd said that you couldn't make it to another season if you hadn't buried what had been plaguing your life in the previous season.

That should have been more than enough food for thought for me, but it wasn't, because I kept doubting my decision to dump Anthony. Pretty stupid, of course. I mean, who was I to question God and His obvious message? Did that make me a bad Christian, if I prayed and worried at the same time? Or did that make me just a vulnerable fool, still tempted to trust two-timing losers?

Hell, I didn't even know if I could trust myself.

The proof was in the pudding. I had walked in on Anthony screwing around with his secretary, so no, he didn't deserve a second chance. As women, we tend to fall in love a little too fast sometimes, I reflected. That perfectly described me, I knew. I'm a Leo, and Leos are strong, mighty, courageous, and—sometimes—stubborn. I had a habit of making up my mind about a man—a first impression—and refusing to let go of that opinion, even when obvious facts proved that my judgment was wrong.

One positive thing I did know about myself, though: I was genuine in every aspect of my life. Men saw that and tore me to shreds. They envisioned a soft soul, one they could come in on and easily take advantage of. I'd had a plan for myself, though, but I'd tossed it out the window at the first offer of a sex-date with Jerome. *Time to get back to the plan, girl,* I told myself.

The night before, I'd spoken with my home girl Bree. She'd moved to Colorado, but we kept in touch. We spoke on the topic of men.

She'd told me I was a great woman and that she was pretty sure any man in the world would want me. I just needed to step back and take a look at myself to see what some of the deeper issues were. Write out the negatives and the positives for each situation. See where the negatives overlapped and try to avoid putting myself in those situations and accepting those things from any new man I'd date.

After the call, I took it all to the Lord in prayer. Looking through the Bible, I came across some verses in Isaiah that talked about the weak renewing their strength in the Lord. I knew as a woman of God that we'd all falter, but that there was Someone stronger who bore it all so that we could each have a second chance at life. Now I had a second chance at love. *"But those who hope in the Lord will renew their strength. They will soar on wings like eagles; they will run and not grow weary, they will walk and not be faint." Isaiah 40:31*

I thought about that list Bree wanted me to make. It could run on for miles. Writing it out seemed silly and laborious. I had to do it, though. I had to for my own sanity, my own health. As I began to think about writing out my list of man wrongs, I arrived at the nail salon.

The girl I'd usually gone to was out. I was already pretty agitated and didn't feel like going to any ole' body. Hell, it was even hard to find a good nail tech these days.

As I realized my mood was flared and my temper was on high, I decided that I'd do the job myself until the following week. While driving home, my mind was racing. A million thoughts fluttered a minute. Thinking about my mistakes with men and that god-awful list was dragging me down.

I made a quick stop at the gas station, stopped at a park, and began to write in my journal. I entitled the list, "A New Beginning." I began to write, and the first thing that came to mind was trust. How could you *EVER* have a healthy relationship if there was no trust? That was surely one of the most important factors in any relationship meant to last.

Besides trust, I wrote "communication, eye contact, and body language." I tended to be a very observant person, so when communicating with people in general, I needed eye contact. It showed me that they respected me, were listening, and were interested in what I had to say.

Men on the other hand, seemed to be good listeners when they wanted to be, but not when it came to correcting their wrongs. I knew that people aren't perfect, and that, at the end of the day, we all, by nature, make mistakes.

The only way to learn from a mistake, especially in a relationship, was to communicate the issues. You'd also have to be confident that the relationship would make it through any situation, given the strength and the willingness of both partners to overcome obstacles.

If my ultimate goal was to get married, I figured I needed to do one thing in particular, and that was to change the way I approached my relationships with men. I also needed to forgive my father for what he had done to my mother all those years ago.

I had to set my standards high and had to keep them that way. I couldn't keep reverting back to the same situations and old behaviors that were keeping me stagnant.

I ripped out the page I'd just written on and started my list over. This time I was going to write from my heart and *NOT* from my overly thinking brain. I realized I needed to get to the root of my own issues and own up to what I needed to fix.

I decided if I would write out this list of what I truly wanted to receive, I could put on my big-girl pants and live out those truths myself. No man I'd ever really deserve was going to show up if I wasn't ready to be the woman for him that I needed to be.

It was time to write out what I wanted to attract as well as to mirror as a woman.

A New Beginning

1. **Trust**—This is a must! You need to trust yourself as well as the other person. Go into your engagements with an open mind and keep in mind that the new guy is *NOT* your old lover. Give him a fair shot until he shows you that he isn't worthy. Please remember to abort the mission at this time because people show you *WHO* they are at the very beginning. Monica, believe them and keep it moving. Make sure that you are being honest and upfront as well. This is not to say that you have to give a guy your complete life's story at the beginning, but always be honest and willing to let your guard down. Relax into love.

2. **Communication**—Say how you feel. Be able to truly open up, when the time is right. Be gentle when discussing matters of the heart, and always take into consideration the other person's feelings. *DON'T* get easily angered because of a disagreement or miscommunication because this will cause you to be your stubborn self, closing off the conversation and running from the responsibility of settling matters. This will lead to tons of open-ended and incomplete conversations that will put a strain on your relationship if not end it.

3. **Openness**—Monica, this is huge! You have always struggled with this. Holding stuff in until it gets to you so badly, that you explode with anger and all sorts of other emotions. When you learn that you can trust your partner, that you two have become exclusive and your lines of communication are intact, it is okay to be open with him about things you may never have wanted to share otherwise. This is therapeutic. Your man (when committed) is your best friend, and if you can trust him with your heart, you can trust him with insecurities or embarrassing issues without feeling like you'll be judged.

4. **Individuality**—Be you, Monica. Don't worry about what he's doing. You need to be honest with yourself. Are you 100% ready for love? If so, that means you're 100% happy with who you see in the mirror, your career and you have your own life outside of Mr. Right. He's there to complement you, not to complete you.

Deal with your unresolved issues before you allow someone into your heart.

5. **Spirituality**—Are you remembering to pray? Are your beliefs and values in alignment with his? This is important, because if you want to have children, you have to think about how that will factor into their lives. Praying is also therapeutic, so if your man isn't on the same page and willing to pray and or doesn't have some sort of spiritual connection, this may go against what you really want.

6. **Standards**—When you set a standard; you need to stick to it. Be sure to also practice what you preach. Don't lower your standards, either—for you or for the guy. If you want a man who saves it for only you, you have to save it for only him.

7. **Respect**—THIS is one of the most important qualities on this list. If you want someone to respect you, you've got to first respect yourself. If you don't give a person something to respect, they will do whatever it is they please. Teach men how to treat you, Monica. This includes expecting faithfulness from a man, and not tolerating any behavior that's less than that, from either of you.

8. **LOVE**—If you want love, you have to be ready to receive it when it presents itself. I know you fear the unknown, but let go of the past and know that the future is far better than what you've ever imagined. Be patient and take your time in love. If it doesn't feel like love, it's probably lust.

9. **Confidence**—Exude this. You are you, Monica. Believe that you are who you are, and that's it. No need to keep being upset or bitter about what some other man did to you or who he left you for. Time heals all broken hearts, but you've got to be willing to let it go. What God thinks about you is the most important thing.

10. **Support**—Does this guy challenge you? Do you challenge him? Are you guys moving in the right direction? You need to stay on your toes and keep him supported as he should you—mentally and emotionally. There is no exception. You should never get

involved with someone and feel more alone than if you'd stayed by yourself. You deserve to have someone who supports you and can be there for you, and vice versa. Don't compromise on this.

I held the journal page close to my chest and gave the thing a hug. I placed it in my bag again so that anytime I forgot what love was supposed to be, I could remind myself.

Ring. Ugh.

As my cell phone rang, I quickly lost concentration.

Jerome was calling, and I really didn't want to talk to him. The thought of that random night, him coming into town and sleeping over, completely disgusted me now. If you gave a guy an inch, he'd be sure to take a mile as long as you allowed it.

I ignored the call and took a deep breath, for I was seriously ready to start from scratch and start the love search again. I was going to be a legit girl from now on. It's the only way I'd ever find and keep a legit man.

I took my journal back out and revisited my list of positives I wanted in a future relationship. I began writing . . . "Don't sleep with a guy before you are committed." That was a big no-no, and I felt like if I called any of my home girls, they'd be able to attest to the reason behind that rule. After all, it was almost like getting med benefits before you'd even earned your first paycheck. As the saying goes, *Why buy the cow, if you can get the milk for free?* No more free milk from me for anybody. Jerome was the type of guy I could never see myself being with anyway.

To me, it was still about the principal of the matter. Sleeping with guys before putting a title on it, made them feel like gods. Who wouldn't want that? Being able to have all the benefits of a woman without commitment, leaving room for them to roam? Don't get me wrong, I'm not bashing a guy for doing such a thing because *WE* women allow it, and *WE* women do it, too! I call that kind of relationship a *dead end.*

Sometimes we all just want to live a little without the actual feeling of having to be committed to one person. Eventually those relationships make for a deadly turn. I say this because we women seem to be emotional creatures by nature. Guys are, too, but they hide their emotions more than we do.

In the friends-with-benefits relationships—or, as I would call them, the dead-end relationships—someone always did the *ULTIMATE* no-no. They would fall in love with the other person. If you are in a strictly friends-with-benefits relationship, then that means there are no feelings involved. How is that possible, though, when humans are made to feel, to love, and to care for one another?

The person that usually fell for the okie-doke first was me. I couldn't seem to help it that I loved hard! Therefore I wrote again:

Horrible Feelings

Broken-hearted and alone is a horrible way to feel.

Most people believe you do it all on your own will.

They believe this because you continue to look for that special someone.

But when you look for them too long, they never come.

It's a horrible way to feel,

Living day after day in your own sins.

In the end, no one ever really wins, except . . .

The one that gets what you've always wanted

Someone to hold her and never let her go

These are horrible feelings, when no one is ever there.

You act as if you don't care, but

You cry yourself to sleep at night,

Trying to see in the dark, but you can't because of your blurred sight.

These are horrible feelings for me

I hope that my heart will soon be set free.

As I continued to reflect on my life and that poem, things became clear to me. I was just making things harder than what they had to be. I had finally set some standards but wasn't yet following my own rules. If I did, maybe things would start looking a little better in the book of love for me.

A Family Affair

9

I'd decided that I'd done enough reflecting for one day and headed home. There was a big day ahead tomorrow, and I needed a clear mind, because I was helping my mom plan for our annual family picnic.

The picnic was always held in St. Louis. My mom would rent a space in Forest Park for the crowd. We had used the same picnic ground for the past few years, and it had become a family favorite. The space was quiet, covered, and even had a great area for games. I'd always appreciated participating, because spending time with family was very important to me.

We had lost four family members within four years, so this year I particularly wanted to be present, for the sake of preserving old memories. I hated the flight from New York to St. Louis, but seeing family that I hadn't seen in a while made the trip so worth it.

Sometimes the distance made it hard for my Mom and I to see eye-to-eye on what foods to make and how the grounds should be set up. I'd like to say it was in her blood to lead with these sorts of events, but a little change and helpful insight from outsiders and past attendees would make for a far better event, if Mom could only be persuaded to be more open. I'd pitched the idea of us having a wish box after this year's picnic. People would be able to state what they liked about the event and what they didn't like. As an effort to make the event *THAT MUCH BETTER* in the years to come, I felt like it was something that was needed.

Since I hadn't grown up with my birth family and I'd had several run-ins with my foster family over the years, it tended to make for awkwardness when "certain" family members came around. But then, who doesn't have family issues? There are *ALWAYS* those few family members who make things a little more difficult. If there wasn't something juicy going on, they didn't want to be there.

I can think of one person in particular who always had to be in the midst of everyone else's frustration. Her name was Cousin Faye. If that woman wasn't the devil himself, I don't know who else she could have been. If there wasn't some gossip to be told, you could find her smiling in people's faces whose backs she had talked behind, or whose husbands she had flirted with.

To be honest, she was pretty low-class, and had a weave that could easily be mistaken for horse hair. Now don't get me wrong—family is family—but if the shoe fits, wear it. I've always been a pretty honest person, so I call it how I see it.

RINNNNGGGG.

The damn phone was driving me crazy. "Can't wait til I'm able to retire and lounge on some black-sand beach," I yelled at it. Running a business and trying to have a normal life easily went hand-in-hand for someone with a nine-to-five, but not for someone whose days were a constant grind.

Of course it was my mom calling, wanting to go over the final list of guests for the picnic. She needed to know who all would be there so there was enough food and refreshments.

Not only was there the family picnic this year, but my sister Renee was due to get the married the exact same day. I didn't want to have to pick and choose between events, so that worked out good for me. I barely made it home to see family anyway since moving to the new city, but working and trying to make time for family and a personal life was getting really complicated.

The wedding wouldn't be until the evening, and the picnic was to take place somewhere around mid-day. I hadn't been home in months, so there were some people I especially wanted to see. Others were more or less invisible in my mind. I say this to mean that they were full of drama and bullshit.

I could never fathom *WHY* some people added being negative to their daily agenda, but hey, I guess that's just how some people are. The family functions would soon turn into a cackling riot upon their arrival. It frustrated me, to say the least, because I didn't like bringing up old dirt. I was finally to a stage in my life where I felt like I had somewhat "arrived."

There was also the peer pressure of me being thirty and *NEVER* having anyone to bring home to the family. "When are you getting married? I'm ready for grandbabies." "Maybe you should try blind dating or hook up with someone online." Please. I mean I loved them all to death, but come on! Everyone's family has problems that need addressing. We had several young'uns with kids, and family members that had been married multiple times, but was I dippin' and dabbin' in the likes and affairs of their lives?

No, I wasn't. I was focused on Monica's business, and it would sure have been nice if they had minded their own business as well. But you have to take the family you are given. Relatives snooping into my business with invasive questions and pressuring advice was as much a part of the annual family picnic as the potato salad. I always went, and I looked forward to it. My purpose for coming was to show some love and support as well as to eat some of that good ole' food.

As far my sister's wedding went, everything had been planned. She'd call me every other day just to make sure I'd be in attendance, and I assured her I would. She seemed so antsy because it was literally days away. It was her special day, and she just wanted to make sure that everything went right.

Yes, I was going to be there. But though my mind was filled with all the melodramas of my sister's wedding and planning the reunion, on a deeper level, something profound was happening in me. I was going to see my father at this picnic, for the first time since Child Welfare Services removed me from my home when I was nine. Now, two decades later, he had stopped drinking, he was in rehab, and he would be attending our family picnic for the first-ever time. He would be attending, and word was out that he wanted to see me.

10

Growing up, I never established a healthy and loving relationship with my father. The only images I had plastered all over my memory involved instability. He wasn't always that way, though. According to my mother, he had been a salesman. In their early twenties, he and my mom together had run a business that brought in hundreds of thousands of dollars each year, and my dad hadn't even completed the ninth grade.

Now that was quite impressive. How could someone go from having so much swag, integrity, and substance to being a raging alcoholic with a drug problem and without even two nickels to rub together? Apparently after his older brother was murdered, he'd had a terrible meltdown. My mother, sisters, and I were just innocent bystanders in the path of his rage. My mom became a punching bag, and my sisters and I became scared shitless. When he was drunk or doped up, we didn't even want to be in his presence.

One night he'd come home in hopes of drinking a Pepsi. There were no more left because my sisters and I had drunk them all. There was no food in the house, so we had just been looking for something that would rid our stomachs of the groaning and cravings for a full-course meal. The Pepsi had been our answer.

He called us into the front room. "All of you, get the hell in here," he yelled, as he stumbled in from the kitchen. "Who the hell drank the last Pepsi?"

In fear of what he might do, none of my sisters answered. Even though we'd split the drink, I didn't want us all going down for the crime. Since I was the oldest, I yelled out that I'd done it. That night, my father took an extension cord to my backside. It took months for the welts to heal. Every time I put on a shirt or pants, I had to do it very slowly to keep from aggravating the wounds.

You see, I was a firm believer in God giving certain battles to His strongest soldiers, but I didn't know if I could forgive something as deep as this. Who the hell wouldn't be angry? If I wasn't as strong as I was, I wouldn't even agree to *TALK TO* his ass. I'd have to face him, though. He would be at the picnic.

While my sisters and I were in the foster care system, we had no contact with our parents whatsoever. A few years ago, one bright and sunny day, I was sitting in my dorm room planning and organizing for my sophomore year in college. I got distracted by a MySpace message from a girl claiming to know my father and mother. I looked at the phone number she sent me for a while and waited a week before calling. I hadn't spoken to or seen my parents in eleven or twelve years, so I assumed someone was toying with me.

Out of sheer curiosity one Friday evening, I picked up my cell and typed in *67 so that my number would appear blocked. The girl that answered the phone was young—I could tell. I asked to speak with my mother, asking for her by her first name.

A voice came over the phone, and my body suddenly grew weak. One thing's for sure, you'll never forget the sound of your mother's voice. I burst into tears, and my mother continued to speak through the phone, hoping to calm me. Finally I settled down, and we had a nice—if somewhat superficial—conversation. So much water had passed under that bridge. You can't just "catch up" with someone you haven't seen in a decade who is the mother you were dragged away from. Finally, after ten or fifteen minutes of chatter, my mom asked if I'd like to speak with "Dad."

"No!" I said, with ice in my voice, all the good feelings I had from conversing with Mom suddenly gone.

"But Monica, he's better now, hon. He wants to talk with you."

"Save it," I said, and hung up.

That phone call had happened years ago. Afterwards, I'd started attending family picnics and getting to know my birth family again. All except for my father. He'd stopped the drugs, I was told, but he was still drinking. I always made sure, before each annual reunion, that *he* would not be there.

But now, he was in rehab, and according to my mom, anxious to make amends. In the Twelve Step Program that recovering alcoholics go through, acknowledging their wrongs and making amends is an essential part of their recovery. I knew alcoholics were supposed to apologize to everyone they had ever hurt, as part of getting better.

Well, that wasn't going to cut it for me. I had no intention of letting that monster corner me at the picnic and start begging, all humble and saint-like, for forgiveness. Because he damn well *WASN'T* going to get it. Damn if I would wipe the slate clean for him, just so he could feel good about his disgusting self. Can you wipe out years of abuse with a friggin' apology? Can you wipe out years of welts on someone's face and backside with an "I'm sorry" smile?

Apologizing so you'll get well is no real apology at all. It's something you do for yourself. Plain selfishness. He wasn't really sorry for what he had done to me and my sisters and mother. He just wanted to be forgiven so he wouldn't have to feel the guilt anymore. I *wanted* him to feel it. I wanted him to be miserable. I told my mom I'd only come to the picnic this year if she *PROMISED* to keep my father away from me.

I had gone to bed and was thinking about all this as I tried to fall asleep. I didn't think about my dad being at the picnic except at night. That's when I couldn't block out my anxiety about him. Would I really be able to avoid him, or would he find a way to corner me?

But something else was upsetting me about all of this: I knew it was wrong of me not to want to forgive. They say you can't truly love yourself as long as you're holding grudges against other people. If I was going to move on and become the Monica I truly wanted to be, the kind of woman who'd attract the legit kind of man I was longing for, I had to do something about my attitude toward my father.

I simply didn't know how to forgive him. How could I possibly do it, when I didn't even want to? I had tried it all. The counseling, mentoring—I even had a spiritual coach, for heaven's sake. This was deep, and I didn't know if I was strong enough to win the battle against the built-up anxiety and hate I had against him. I hated it every time I looked in the mirror because I saw images and traces of him in me. From the way I smiled to the way I raised my chin. How do you ever love yourself when you look like the person you hate above everything?

Feeling overwhelmed with it all, the picnic three days away, I got out of bed and down on my knees. I bent my head and talked to God. There was only one thing I wanted from Him, and that was to take the pain away. It was making me sick! I looked healthy on the outside, but when I went home at night and my head hit that pillow, it was almost like I'd died. All I needed was for someone to place coins over my eyes so that I could pay Charon, the mythological ferryman that carried souls into the pits of Hades! Geesh—that's what my life felt like, a living hell. And I knew if God was going to take the pain away, I had to be willing to do my part. I had to be *willing* to forgive. *God, make me willing.*

Suddenly the phone rang. Who would be calling me at such a crazy hour? Caller ID showed my mother's number. She must have forgotten it's two hours later here than where she lives. I got off my knees, picked up the phone, and muttered, "Hi, Mom."

"Monica? This is Dad."

The moment his deep voice murmured through the receiver, a bubbling took over my stomach. My insides felt like a volcano getting ready to erupt. The anger I'd buried all those years came drenching down my face in the form of sweat. My heart was pounding, and my eyes were tearing up. The tears were a combination of sad, angry, and painful feelings that I thought I'd gotten over but were obviously still there to deal with.

"Sweets, I wanted to talk to you," he said quietly through the phone. That was a name he'd given me when I was a young child, and him calling me that made me even angrier. There was nothing sweet about the way we had to grow up. Flashbacks of my mom's brutal beatings, and my own, blurred my vision. It was almost as if a horror movie was playing, uninvited, inside my head.

The sound of his voice just irritated the hell out of me. Since I'd had a conversation with myself and the good ole' Lord, I decided it was time for me to get real with this man. I was going to *HAVE* this conversation with the sonofabitch, and respond authentically.

"How has everything been going, Sweets? I see you're out of school and running your own business now. I'm really proud of you for that," he said.

"Stop calling me 'Sweets,'" I said. "You've no right to call me that." I yelled through the phone that I felt like he'd ruined me and that there was no man that would ever want me because I was tainted, beat-up, and bruised. I hated that I was carrying all that baggage, but you know what, I was ready to stop playing victim, I said. I was ready to hear him once and for all say he was wrong and that he'd take responsibility for his horrible parenting.

In my mind, I told him, he wasn't a parent at all. His sole and only purpose was to place my sisters and me here on this earth so that we could become advocates for victims of abuse. We'd be strong, and we'd all one day fall in love with the men of our dreams and have beautiful healthy families. In *SPITE* of him, I added with spite!

No, I was no victim. I was a victor. I was Monica Walker—magazine owner. I lived in a loft in New York, and I drove a Jag. I was strong, confident, and radiant. My mere presence brought joy to my employees. I didn't need alcohol or drugs to get through life, like he did. I was happy, healthy, and waiting on love. I was ready to be swept off my feet, and I damned sure deserved all the good that was getting ready to come to me.

By the time I finished saying all that, I was breathing heavily. I sat down on the bed to listen to whatever it was he had to say. For a moment, all I heard was silence.

"Monica," he said at last, "I am so sorry for what I did to you, your mom, and sisters. It wasn't right. The alcohol and drugs have ruined me, and until this day, as a man, I can never forgive myself. You all are beautiful creatures that should be loved on and taken care of, and it seems all I did was ruin the insides of you all. Monica, I'm not expecting you to forgive me. I'm grateful that you'll even sit here and have a conversation with me because none of your sisters want to have anything to do with me. I was young, stupid, and a terrible father. I would be dead today if any man ever laid hands on any of y'all, because of what I'd do to him. Now, I know what you're thinking, '*I need to take in what I'm preaching,*' but Sweets, it's too late. What's done is done, and I am just so proud of the beautiful, strong, and ambitious woman that you are today. You are going to go far. You deserve the world, and I'm going to pray to God that He brings you a man that makes and keeps you abundantly happy. Please forgive me, Sweets, because now that I'm older, I understand that what I did was wrong. I want to be there to help you through whatever it is that you have going on in your life—with men . . . you name it. Please just give me that opportunity."

As he spoke, I couldn't help but get weak on the inside. My sweet and kindred heart had a mind of its own. My heart now wanted to forgive him, but a bigger part of me held firmly onto my rage. I just wasn't willing to let the past go. How *COULD* I?

"I've got to go now, Dad," I said in a hoarse voice. I was surprised to hear "Dad" coming out of my mouth.

"I understand, Monica. I hope we'll see each other at the picnic."

I hung up the phone without saying goodbye.

I had a mentor once tell me that I could look at the past as something really bad that happened to me and continue to live there, by allowing my mind to replay its imagery *OR* I could say to myself, "Look, by comparison, at where you are now."

I was ready to pay attention to where I was now and move forward. One thing's for sure: most families that got separated like we did still were in search of one another. But we were the lucky ones—brought back into each other's lives to mend things or ignore the chance, however we decided. I began to believe that my father appearing in my life again, at this very moment, was destiny. His words had sounded sincere, so desperate and broken. I finally wanted to forgive him.

I pulled out my journal and went in.

The Child with All the Heart

Once a lost spirit, a lost soul

Waiting to be reborn again and made whole

From growing up in a drug-infested house

To graduation day and buying my own first couch,

I was living a life of complete dissatisfaction

. . . and in that I'd manifest a reaction to love.

I didn't know how to accept it, obtain it,

Explain it, or give it.

I neglected it.

I left it—love—standing in the cold

Until I went to church one Sunday and asked Jesus to make me whole again

Put me at peace, and my spirit ease.

In those trying times, I wept and I cried

Until my heartbeat paced slower and those cries became sighs.

I didn't share my feelings. To the world I was just some little lost girl

Another case number on some social worker's desk,

Waiting to be birthed into livelihood at eighteen,

A god-awful mess.

I took the leap of faith with dignity and a pen attached to my hand

Because by them I knew I would never be abandoned.

They kept me grounded

Even when the walls were closing in and I was surrounded.

Full of emotions and frustration, I was trapped and stressed

With some serious internal mess that needed to be addressed.

I held my eyes to Thine hills, and Jesus spoke to me.

He told me to let it all out . . . to be free.

To this day, I am free

Through Him my mind, spirit, and body redeemed.

I have suffered, but now I live the life I was meant to live

Free-spirited and by His will.

I could be upset. I could live my life out forever as a victim. I could stay up all night angry at the world because my inner child is mad she didn't have a daddy. I could walk around all day with my arms folded and roll my eyes at any being of the opposite sex. I could sulk. I could decide that there is really not too much to be happy for in life. I could continue to bury the pain underneath my heart. What does this prove, though? What internal issues would I be solving? Guess what: none. This is why I love journaling. There is no judgment, just acceptance. I wish people were like that.

My father is a great man, and I can tell. Sometimes people do just get really messed up, right? I mean some people get so messed up that it's too late for them. Well, I hope it's not too late for my father and me. I'm a traveler on this road to love, and a father has the key that every daughter needs. It unlocks that internal self-love and self-confidence that most women without fathers don't have—well, except the really strong ones, like me. For me, I just need to forgive and move on. I am so ready to do that. I know that the man of my dreams is out there and that the One above has used His best tools to sculpt him . . . just for me. Well, it's getting late. I'm grateful for this journal. I'm glad it will always be there when I need it . . . just pen, paper, and the universe.

After I wrote those last words, I stuck the notebook in a nightstand drawer and turned out the light. I slept well that night, for the first time in a long while.

Vergil

11

I'd finally packed my suitcase for the flight to St. Louis. There was so much pressure between work and commuting through the city every day that I was in desperate need of a vacation. I had a great crew for the magazine, but one guy that couldn't write a lead to save his life. To top it off, he had a dysfunctional family—which I suppose made us members of the same club.

As I sat in my office sorting through a blizzard of emails, there was a knock at the door. It was Blake.

"Blake, please not right now," I said.

"Well, there's someone here to see you. He says he's an old friend and has some ideas about a new magazine venture."

"Huh. Okay. Send him in, I guess."

As I sat there with a slouch that was worse than an old woman's, the door crept open.

I couldn't believe it. Vergil Thomas!

He stood about six-fee-two and had warm, deep-brown eyes and dark, smooth skin. His suit was tailored so well you could almost see that he was a regular visitor to the gym. His stance was relaxed, and his smile was amazing. Just as I'd remembered it.

Trying to recover from my surprise and establish a professional manner, I stood and held out my hand.

He reached over with his long arms and hugged me instead. "Come on, Monica. You know I don't do handshakes when it comes to you," he said.

Vergil and I had become very close in college. He was cute and smart. He had a great personality, but I always looked at him as a lab partner or study buddy—a friend. I couldn't really wrap my mind around us ever being anything more.

Plus he was very quiet and kept to himself. He never even tried to ask me out—even though he'd made it known he had a thing for me!

I'd heard that after college, Vergil had gone on to attend medical school. It was always his dream to become a doctor. He was very fond of helping others and was pretty much a stand-up kind of guy. I always knew he'd be something great. I just didn't think he would pop back into my life, and so suddenly.

"How have you been?" he asked with a mischievous grin.

"I see now," I said, crossing my arms. "'I have an idea for your magazine' was just some line to get through the door."

"Well, I had to find some way to get past the pit bulls."

By pit bulls, Vergil meant the top-heavy security guards stationed at the front of the building.

I was so nervous that I didn't even think to offer the man a seat. He sat down anyway, and I went back to my desk. I couldn't help being mesmerized by his looks. I didn't remember him being so handsome. His eyes were daunting, and that jaw line was to die for. His lips looked kissable, and his arms looked like they could protect a small village.

"I've been fine, just very busy here is all. How have you been?" I asked.

"I've been well. I found out you were in New York through Larry—remember him? I thought I'd stop by since I was in town."

"Oh. Well, that was nice of you," I said.

My office was becoming hot, and my reaction time was off. I felt exhausted, like I hadn't been to bed in days. Vergil kept eyeing me, waiting for my next response, but I was so drawn to him that I was at a loss for words.

"I was headed to lunch if you'd like to join me," I finally said.

"I'd love that," he answered.

As I grabbed my purse, I could feel his eyes on me. I became very conscious of what I was wearing—a pencil skirt and a crisp cotton blouse. My heels were high enough to show I was a woman but low enough to keep my feet from barking by day's end. Yes, I thought I looked okay. I hoped so.

He took my jacket down off from the wall and politely opened the door. We bumped each other and as I turned around, and our eyes met. Then I stepped back, bumped into my desk, and a stack of files tumbled to the floor, all the contents spilling onto the carpet.

Vergil rushed in to help me pick up the mess. His closeness was making me sweat.

"I'm so clumsy sometimes," I said, embarrassed as hell. When had he become so good-looking?

I watched him hungrily as he picked up the last folder. When he stood up, I quickly turned toward my desk, pretending to look for something.

"You ready to head out, Miss Walker?" he asked.

"I'm ready now," I giggled.

As we stood by the elevator, there was an awkward silence. I suddenly wondered if maybe Vergil was as nervous as I was. We both began to speak at once, which made us both laugh. That broke the tension a little.

On the way down, I stared at the floor numbers. It seemed to take forever for the elevator to descend. I could feel Vergil's eyes examining me. A daydream crashed into my head of Vergil stopping the elevator and grabbing me in his arms, professing his heartfelt love ever since college. I had to get hold of myself!

Walking out of the elevator, I straightened my blouse and smoothed my skirt.

"What hospital are you stationed at, Vergil? Are you in Atlanta?" I asked.

"Yep, still there. I started out at Grady, but then I moved over to the ER section at Emory Crawford Long."

"Man, you're doing well for yourself, I must say." I smiled.

When we got to the deli, we took a seat at the table closest to the exit. Vergil asked if I wanted anything to drink.

"I'll just have bottled water," I said, and he went up to get drinks for us from the serving line.

While Vergil walked away, my mind went back to college, and I tried to remember how we had first met. I thought it was in a science class, but couldn't quite remember. He was a little nerdy back then but smart, and he looked like a few wardrobe changes and a haircut could get him right. Well, time since then had made him more than right. Vergil was fine. I couldn't believe he was this handsome and single! Or was he? I had just assumed, the way we seemed to be flirting . . .

"Vergil, are you still single?" I blurted out when he came back.

"Yes," he said with a laugh. "How about you?"

"Oh, yes," I said, trying to sound coy, but failing miserably. He laughed again. It was pretty clear that I liked him.

We went through the line and got our lunches. The deli wasn't a romantic place, but it was the restaurant closest to the office, and I had to get back for a staff meeting in an hour. I apologized to Vergil for the less than charming ambience, and explained about my meeting.

"No worries," he said. "I'm just glad you could make time for me, the way I barged in unannounced and all. I have to leave soon myself to catch my return flight. But I'm hoping I can see you again when I come back next month."

"Next month?" I said, surprised.

"I expect to be in New York quite a bit, now that Larry is opening up a medical office here. We're starting a practice here together."

"Oh, wow. That's great! I think you guys can do it. I mean, New York is a great place to be—as long as you have a little money and a dream," I said.

My heart had started pounding. Vergil was moving here! I wouldn't date a guy long-distance, but if he was moving here, Vergil might be a real legit-man possibility.

I couldn't believe this dude was still single. But then, he'd always kept to himself in college most of the time, focusing on school work rather than on the girls. He wasn't like the other guys, the guys I was busy chasing.

We spent lunch catching up on our lives. I had forgotten how smart Vergil was. His vocabulary could blow a dictionary away. He was constantly using words I didn't recognize, but I batted my eyes and pretended like I did.

"Well, Ms. Monica, I have your card. I'll call you," he said, when we got back to my workplace and stepped off of the elevator. He leaned down, and instead of offering a handshake or friendly hug, he landed a kiss right on my cheek. The heat of his breath made me close my eyes, and I exhaled. I didn't know why that moment felt so right; it just did.

As Vergil walked away, I smiled and waved. When I got back to my office, my heart was still pounding. It was like Vergil was there. I was at an all-time high! I was finally getting over the Anthony and the Jerome situations. Vergil popping up made those men seem like dust in a universe of stars.

I mean he was amazing! I didn't see how I could have ever missed that while in college. Now that the wool was pulled back from my eyes, I was ready for a new venture . . . in all aspects of my life.

That day I made a vow to myself: If Vergil and Larry truly started a practice here, I was so going to go for it. I was going to have Vergil as my man. I mean, I would have been crazy to let that opportunity pass me up *AGAIN*, right?

I told my assistant to gather the staff together for our meeting. I put the papers that had tumbled onto the floor back into their proper files, and grabbed the materials needed for my PowerPoint presentation.

As the staff filed into the conference room, Blake was fidgety as usual. Maybe it's because he knew I knew what he was capable of, so I held him to a very high standard. He was even the one in charge whenever I left for a trip.

"Hey team, how is everyone doing this afternoon?" I asked. "I know it's late in the week, but I want you guys to get amped because we are officially launching our third issue this month!"

Everyone applauded, and I walked toward my PowerPoint presentation. I pulled up the slides for them all to see, and the meeting began.

"Today I want to do things a little differently," I told them. I know when we first started, I assigned a few hands to come on board to lay out *ALL* the details of what would be in each issue, and we assigned you guys particular tasks, depending on your skillsets. Well, today, I don't want to do that. I wouldn't have hired you all if I didn't feel you were capable of getting the job done and doing it well. So for this particular issue, I want each team to get together and brainstorm for a particular section they'd like to see in the magazine. I want it to be new . . . fresh . . . innovative."

The teams pulled together, and excited murmurs permeated the room.

"I have to catch a flight tomorrow," I said, interrupting. "I'm headed to St. Louis for a family function. Therefore the capable Blake will be overseeing all tasks until my return on Monday. Tomorrow morning I want to meet with everyone so we can discuss what each of your teams came up with. We'll incorporate it into the PowerPoint, cutting out what we don't need so that we can get started. Any questions?"

I scoped the room for raised hands, but none appeared. I gathered my items and headed for the door. Victoria, who worked in PR, came scurrying after me. She was always one to have questions. I turned to her and smiled.

"Hi, Victoria, what may I help you with?"

"Um, actually I was hoping I could show you something. Can we speak in private, though?"

"What's going on?" I asked, once we both had sat down in my office.

"So, this is kind of personal, and I never really wanted to bring it up, but I have an idea for one of the teams to work on, or maybe I could work on it myself," she said.

She laid a binder in front of me.

"What's this?"

"It's my idea," she said.

I looked through each page, and the idea was brilliant. Not only was it brilliant, but it hit close to home for me. Victoria had grown up in a foster home, as I had. She wanted to add a part to the family section that spoke to adoption, foster youth, and how people could donate and help. The section would also highlight free programs that provided mentoring, helping foster care youth with college and life after the system.

"I love it. This is great!"

Victoria let out a sigh of relief. She held her chest and grinned.

"Thank you so much! This really means a lot to me," she said.

Victoria explained that she had a dream to one day start a nonprofit organization geared toward mentoring. It was her passion to find a way to do more for youth who seem to get abandoned when it came to making healthy decisions and planning for the future.

"This hits home for me because I grew up in a similar situation," I said, "and I believe any news coverage that brings awareness to the foster care issue would be fabulous. So for that, I thank you. I'd be happy to incorporate your concept into the magazine."

I looked at Victoria, and another thought came to mind.

"I have an idea of my own," I said. "What about having you scope the city for individuals who are very successful and who might like to share their success stories with others, with young people like yourself who are looking to win in business and in life?"

"I don't think I understand," Victoria said.

"Well, I'm thinking I'd pay for a speakers to come here once a month to speak to the staff on their successes and what they did to get to where they are. This could be helpful for everyone and also would help keep the office upbeat and in a state of enthusiasm about the magazine. I'll discuss this with the team when I get back, so meanwhile it's our secret," I said.

I escorted Victoria to the door. "I'll pass your idea along to Blake and have him assign it to one of the people who work on the family section," I said. "If you want to help, I'll let him know that you're more than welcome. Expertise is golden."

She smiled and left. I headed to my desk and flopped down in my chair. I smiled, knowing that I'd had done a good deed, without letting on too much about my own personal tragedies.

When I finally arrived home after a long day, my phone rang, and it was Vergil. I smiled and let it go to voicemail. I was tired and had a lot to get done for the weekend trip to St. Louis.

St. Louis

12

Finally, Friday afternoon and I was on the plane, headed to St. Louis. I had my carryon bag, purse, and laptop for emails. As a business owner, I had literally no days off.

I sat in my assigned seat and waited for the rest of the people to board. When the last passenger took his seat, the flight attendant started with her safety routine.

As the plane pulled out, the captain came over the intercom. "We may experience some slight turbulence en route to St. Louis," he said. "The weather will be rainy and a little cold. Fifty-five degrees there at the moment. Not quite what you'd expect for a summer day. Hope everyone's buckled up and ready to go. The fasten-seatbelt sign has been turned on."

The plane took off, and I was ready to fall asleep. The air was on high, and the lady who sat next to me was already dead to the world and snoring. I wanted to sleep, but decided I couldn't. I had so much work to do, and my mind was always running a million miles a minute whenever I had to leave "nervous-wreck Blake" in charge. He was always worried. I knew he was capable—I just needed him to relax. When he was nervous, I was nervous.

In spite of myself, I drifted off, and awoke to the captain's announcement that we had arrived in St. Louis. He announced the current temperature and said we could now use our cellular devices.

I stretched and reached under my seat and into my bag to grab my phone. The first person I wanted to call was my cousin Millie. She was so cool and laid back. I'd be staying with her over the weekend. She said if I phoned her when I landed, she'd meet me at the baggage claim. I knew if I could depend on her. She was a great friend.

Millie was tall and slender. She was the sweetest glass of lemonade on hot summer day. She had sass, smarts, and a no-nonsense personality. She always spoke what was real. If you didn't want to hear the truth, she was the last one you'd want to approach. That's what I admired about her.

I walked through the crowded airport looking for the terminal that led to ground transportation. When I arrived, Millie was already out front waiting for me.

"Just in time," I grinned.

"Girl, come on. It is *FREEZING* out here," she said.

"This is crazy weather. I can't believe this. That global warming must really be taking its toll on poor ole' St. Louis," I said.

As we drove off, I smiled. I was happy to be home, to see family and to enjoy what little time I'd be here. I was sure hoping that the weather was going to be nice.

All I knew was that I was ready for some good food, family, games, and catching up. I knew my father would be there, but that wasn't bothering me like it did before. I was finally ready to face him.

We pulled up to Millie's house and parked in the garage. I grabbed my belongings and followed her to the guest room. It was nice! It had a very serene and spa-like feel. The walls were matted with the perfect shade of brown, and the lights were low-lit. A few corners provided a safe haven for plants, and the bathtub looked like it belonged in a master bedroom. I was in heaven. This was so much better than the small and cramped apartments New York had to offer.

It was comparatively peaceful in St Louis. The streets of New York ran all hours of the night, so I was sure to hear a train passing, the honking of taxis, playful kids, or the trash man chasing away the city's big rats in an effort to pick up trash at three a.m.

Here it was different. I felt a sense of calm over Millie's house, and that was something I had been away from for quite some time. This was perfect.

"Monica!" Millie was calling me from the second floor. "Are you hungry?"

Her voice was muffled but I could still make out what she was asking. I yelled back.

"I'll let you know in a couple of hours," I said.

It had gotten late, and all I wanted to do was go to bed, but that would be impolite. I needed to spend some time with Millie.

"We should hit the mall in the morning," I yelled up to her, as I unpacked. "I need to find something to wear for the picnic."

"Yeah—me, too. I was thinking the same thing. We should probably check the weather before we head out. Gotta be prepared for anything in this bi-polar weather."

I went into the living room, and Millie met me there. We both flopped down on the couch.

"Hey, whatever happened to that guy Anthony you were emailing me about?" she said. "I haven't heard you mention the likes of him in some time."

"That's been over," I said. "Girl, that was on some straight waiting-to-exhale shit. I couldn't believe the drama. He was handsome, a big-time sales executive, and he worked in one of the elite office buildings in New York. He drove a Maserati, smelled good, and kissed like a true lover," I said.

"Well, what the hell happened?"

To tell the rest of the story, I fluffed a pillow in my arms and pulled my legs up under me.

"To make a long story short, he was a no-good, two-timing loser. He slept with his assistant in the middle of the day, and I walked in on it."

Millie's eyes grew big in the disbelief.

"Girl, shut the front door!" she said.

As Millie sat up, I shook my head and shrugged my shoulders.

"Girl, I'm definitely not tripping off that because I'm on to the next best thing. I'm not wasting any more time." I said.

"Let me tell you something, cousin," said Millie. "You are a phenomenal woman. God is going to send you someone, believe me. When He does, that man is going to be head-over-heels in love with you. Shoot, if I was a man and single, *I'D* date you."

I lay back on the couch and put my hand on my forehead.

"Aw, come on. No need to be hard on yourself. I'm telling you this because I know. I went through the same thing, and I continued until I trusted God. Girl, I wasn't even looking for my husband. He just showed up one day. Now I can't get rid of him. Sometimes I want to stamp a sign on his forehead that says 'return to sender.'" She laughed.

Millie got up and walked to the kitchen. "You want a glass of wine?"

"Sure. Why the hell not?" We moved our conversation to the kitchen.

"So, like I was saying, you let God make a man out of him before you make him a husband. You know you *CAN'T* raise a man, because he's already grown. If he don't want it, you can't make nobody—I heard that off a K. Michelle track. A woman should be so buried and lost in God that a man has to seek Him to get to her, or however that saying goes. Maya Angelou brought that one about."

I placed my elbows on the counter and took a sip from my wine glass. My cousin was making some great points, and I was listening carefully. She was a smart woman, and I knew it. Heck, she was happily married, so I was pretty sure she wasn't just telling me all of this for the hell of it.

"Okay, lady. Well, thanks for the advice. I definitely hear what you're saying and I have taken mental notes," I told her.

"Well, I'm going to head to bed. We'll want to get to the mall early so we make it in time for the picnic."

"I'm with you on that." We parted ways and walked to our separate rooms.

I sat on my bed and grabbed my laptop. I answered some emails from Blake, then picked up my cell phone and noticed I had a missed call from Vergil.

Hey, it's Vergil, the message said. *Just wanted to make sure you got to St. Louis safe and sound, my beautiful queen. Have a great night.*

As the message ended, I clenched the phone to my chest. Vergil definitely seemed like he was one in a million, but I maybe I had passed judgment too quickly. I seemed to have a bad habit of doing that.

I made a mental note to call him when I touched down in New York. I was here to enjoy my family and some old friends, not spend this time thinking about men.

But not thinking about men was actually kind of impossible. After all, finding the right one had become so important to me. How could I not think about it? I tried to sleep, but decided I needed to write. Maybe that would clear my head, and then I could settle down.

I sat up, turned on the light, and grabbed my journal:

> *Life and all its experiences are making me a little better. As I sit*
> *here on my bed and put pen to paper, I'm turning on my dream*
> *machine and envisioning a man who will be head-over-heels in*
> *love with me. I've been attracting all the wrong sorts, and I don't*
> *know if the repetitive cycles are from childhood memories or IF*
> *I'm just too gullible and blind to see people for what they really*
> *are. I mean, I even lost several friends—or people I thought to*
> *be friends—when I started my magazine and they got jealous.*
> *It was like they never had had my best interests in mind, and*
> *I sometimes feel it's that way with men—like they're all so selfish*
> *and inconsiderate. I don't mean to bash them, and I try not to*
> *think negative and make stereotyped judgments about men in*
> *general, but sometimes it's hard not to do. After all, I spent my*
> *twenties dealing with all the wrong guys. No matter how old*
> *they got, the same behavior was present. Am I really thirty now?*
> *You'd sure never know it by the likes of some of the men I've been*
> *attracting. I guess age isn't anything but a number, but guys are*
> *going to have to show me a little bit more than what I've been*

finding all these years. I am ready to meet someone who accepts me with all my flaws, and I accept them with theirs. I'm ready for late nights by the fire, wine, and endless cuddling with someone who truly cares about me. I'm ready to face life with my true love by my side, to support my man and be his rock when the times get tough. I'm ready to trade the single life for a ring and a family.

The next morning I awoke to my alarm clock. It was 8:00 a.m. I rolled out of bed and reached for my slippers. I peeped down the hall to see if Millie was sleeping, but her door was closed, so I guessed her husband had come in the night after we were already in bed.

I splashed water onto my face and brushed my teeth. Before I hit the shower, I raised the window to see what the temperature felt like. It was still a little nippy, and I couldn't believe that! I felt so ready to throw on a cool summer dress.

By the time I finished my shower, I could smell of the aroma of pancakes and bacon. I closed my eyes and smiled as I breathed in the aroma. Most of my mornings, all I had time for was a piece of cold toast, fruit, and a cup of coffee, if I was lucky.

When I got downstairs, Millie was at the stove. "Good morning, girl. How did you sleep last night?"

"Like a baby," I said.

I didn't get many good nights of sleep. They didn't mix with late office hours and very early mornings, so Lord knows I was in heaven. Even if it was only for a weekend, I couldn't get the smile to leave my face.

"Well, I've got bacon, eggs, hash browns, fruit, and pancakes. You're welcome to any of it," Millie smiled.

"Aw cousin, that was too sweet. You didn't have to do all that," I said.

"Girl, don't worry. I know you rarely get mornings like this."

When we finished eating, we headed to the mall. Sifting through the clothes started to give me a headache. The stores were just too busy. I'd be looking for an item, then someone would see me there and rudely start sifting through the same row. I was beyond irritated. I grabbed a pair of Levi jeans and a nice dress blouse with a leather jacket and called it day.

I waited for Millie to finish, and we headed out.

"So are you ready for today?" she asked.

"As ready as I'm going to be."

We pulled into her driveway and rushed to get our clothes on. Millie had made potato salad and a couple of apple pies, and we packed those into the car.

I checked the forecast, and rain was coming our way.

"Do you think people will come to the picnic if it rains?" I asked.

"Rain, sleet, or snow, you know this family is going to stick to their outings," she answered.

As we drove through the city and down to the park, my heart dropped into my stomach. I couldn't believe what I was seeing. There were so many vacated and burned-downed buildings. The church I'd attended while growing up was still intact, but to look at the surrounding area almost brought tears to my eyes.

When Millie and I arrived at the park, my mom and a few others were already there setting up camp. In the back of my mind I was hoping my cousin Sam didn't show up.

Sam had married my cousin Gwen, and he had a reputation for flirting with female family members. There were just certain lines that should *NEVER* be crossed, and Sam liked to cross them.

"Hi, Mom," I said.

"*AHHHHH!* Sweetie, how are you doing?" she said, giving me a huge hug. "Look at you—so beautiful! I'm so proud. New York must be treating you well."

Mom looked pretty good herself, and I told her so. It felt great to see her again.

Just as I got ready to sit down, thunder struck and a heap of rain poured down. Luckily we were in a covered area. Some of the napkins and plastic condiments began to fly all over the picnic grounds.

When the storm subsided, we retrieved what we could, as several more family members arrived. Aunt Patty and Uncle Earl, a few of my cousins, and—Sam and Gwen. The sight of him made me feel sick to my stomach.

By now our picnic area was packed. The sun was showing up and shining warmly. Maybe we'd get a good picnic day after all.

Last to arrive were my sister Renee and Miles, her husband-to-be. Renee was full of smiles and chattering excitedly about their wedding, which was to take place in the evening. I liked the looks of the groom. He wasn't just handsome. There was something solid and strong about him that was hard to put into words. His eyes followed Renee wherever she went, as if, to him, she was the only woman in the park.

Just before everyone sat down to say a prayer of blessing, a familiar voice rang out. It was my father.

I felt a lump in my throat. My bottom went cold, and my adrenaline began to pump. My heart was beating in my ears, and my hands were shaking. As he walked in my direction, I turned to speak to an aunt who was beside me, pretending I didn't see him.

Then he stepped right up to me and said, "Hey, Sweets."

"Hi. How have you been?"

"You want to take a walk with me?"

I swallowed and followed him in the direction of his truck. I leaned against it as he searched for the words he wanted to say.

"Look, Sweets. I'm sorry," he said.

"I forgive you," I blurted out before he could say anything else.

"Really?" he said, surprised.

"Yes. I can't spend the rest of my life holding a grudge against you, because it's not healthy. What's done is done, and I've come to accept that. Let's get back to the picnic," I said.

In that moment, my father gripped me in his arms and held me tighter than a cuddled pillow. He actually cried. I wrapped my arms around him and held him until he stopped. I couldn't help but feel moved. Finally, he pulled away, kissed me on the forehead, and we returned to the tables.

The family sat down, ate, joked, and laughed together. We shared old memories and talked about some of our goofy family traditions. One of these was watching The Temptations movie on Thanksgiving and Christmas. We were pure old-school. The VHS tape had been watched so many times that some parts skipped when it played.

The day went on, the children raced off to the playground equipment, and the card games began. Just as the day was beginning to be marked as a great one, a scream rang out from the ladies' restroom.

Millie came marching out, furious. Following her was Sam and our twenty-one-year-old cousin, Sadie. Millie had walked in on them having sex!

All of the family members who had small children headed to their cars and exited the park. My mom and I rushed to pack away all picnic items, along with help from other family members.

The picnic grounds that had been filled with laughter, smiles, good food and drinks, had turned into a cloud-covered, cold, and vacant lot. The family was now scarce, and the ones who were left whispered in disgust and disappointment.

I said my last goodbyes. Millie and I headed for the car and then home.

There was an awkward silence for a moment, and then Millie made a sudden turn into a gas station.

"Can you believe that shit!? I mean, I am still sitting here trying to wrap my brain around what happened. What the fuck is wrong with that boy?" she seethed.

I'd never heard Millie use such profane language before, so I knew she was mad.

"That boy needs to get a hobby. Every time we have a family function, it always comes to an abrupt end because of something Sam does. Sadie should be a shamed of herself," she said. "Poor Gwen! How does the woman put up with it?"

"Girl, I am sitting here in as much disbelief as you are."

The rest of the ride home was quiet. The rain had made us sleepy, and the day's events were enough to make anyone want to spend some time alone.

When Millie and I got to the house, we went to our separate rooms. Millie didn't say too much more that day, and I barely saw her.

Even though I was tired, I still had to muster up enough energy to make an appearance at my sister's wedding at 7:30 that evening. I couldn't picture myself staying late since I'd already had a pretty eventful and dramatic day. My emotions where all over the place, and office matters were plastered at the forefront of my mind.

I answered emails for a while, then crashed on the bed until my alarm clock rang. Around 6:45, I walked down the hall and knocked on Millie's door. She appeared to be sleeping, but I needed to borrow her car to drive to the wedding.

I got the keys from her, and climbed into the car, hoping I wouldn't be late. I drove down Natural Bridge until I spotted the church off to the right.

When I walked inside, most of the guests were already seated, so I crept in, grabbing a spot in back. I didn't want to take one of the few remaining double-seats, because couples might arrive, or people with guests, who would need to sit there.

The set-up of the venue was exquisite. My sister Renee had always had a thing for lavender, so that's what the church was draped in. There were candles and bouquets and a white bridal carpet down the center aisle. Organ music played softly in the background.

After the last few guests arrived and the pastor and groom had taken their places in front, the bridesmaids and groomsmen marched in. There were four of each. The flower girl—one of our nieces—followed behind, shyly dropping rose petals down the aisle.

When the organist began to play the traditional wedding anthem, everyone rose, and my sister appeared at the back of the church, on the arm of our proud-looking father. Her eyes were filled with joy, and she looked absolutely stunning. She wore a long white dress, halter-topped, with a sleek train in back.

The pastor asked us to be seated as he joined the two in matrimony. I couldn't believe that my sister was younger than me and had already found her man. Even from the back of the church, you could see the light in his eyes whenever he looked at her. What I wouldn't give to be bathed in that kind of devotion.

It seemed as if the wedding started and ended in the blink of an eye. I kissed Renee and my new brother in law, congratulating them on their union. I followed the crowd to the reception but was so exhausted that I only stayed a few minutes.

When I finally arrived back at Millie's, the house was dark and quiet. I tiptoed up the stairs, showered, and fell into a dead sleep as soon as my body hit the sheets.

The next morning, I awoke at 5:00 a.m. "Geesh, can I just get one day to actually sleep in?" I muttered to myself, irritated. I knew I couldn't go back to sleep, so I opened my laptop to check emails. There were several from Blake, a few from Veronica, and looka' here, one from Anthony.

I almost didn't open it. Sure enough, it was just about what I expected:

> *Good morning, Sunshine. Look, I feel really bad about what I did to you. I know that you are probably hurting [I wasn't], probably crying [wrong again], and probably never want to speak to me again [right for once]. I've never felt the way I feel for you about any other woman. That beautiful smile you have, your sense of humor, the many talents you possess, the sweetness in your eyes, the mere innocence that I saw every time I looked at you, and the way you made my heart smile. My mother never brought me up to be such a horrible example, and I'm sure my grandmother is during somersaults in her grave, disapproving of what I have done. I wish I could go back in time and change it. I feel like I took an excellent example of a woman for granted, and now I have to live with the regret of losing you. If you could ever find it in your heart to forgive me . . .*

I was so fed up and irritated with Anthony that I didn't see the point in even finishing his email. I mean, these guys, *MOST*, were all the same. Ya' got something good to take home to mama, but you're constantly chasing what you feel is the next best thing. I didn't have time for that, and I didn't have an ounce of sympathy in me for Anthony. He had brought all of that on himself.

I deleted the email and checked the one from Veronica. She had another question about the magazine launch. I replied, checked the emails from Blake, and rolled myself out of bed and onto the floor. My flight was due to leave in a few hours. I wanted to make some last visits to family before I left.

Millie was still in bed, so I lightly knocked on the door and asked if I could borrow the car for a bit. She responded with a grunt that I took for a yes, and I headed out.

I stopped for breakfast at IHOP. When I was walking out, an older man touched my elbow and said, "Woman, you are heaven-sent. If I was half my age, I'd be married to you now. Your husband is one lucky man."

I responded with a fake smile and walked to the car. As I drove, I thought about all the many things I could have done differently that might have landed me Mr. Right.

When I got to my mom's house, a lot of my cousins and aunts were there. Mom asked where Millie was, and I told her she was still asleep.

As we enjoyed the rest of our time together, I felt all mushy and warm inside. Family sure was a great way to stay happy. This visit had been worth it, in spite of Sam.

When I got back to Millie's, she was ready to take me to the airport. We packed up and headed out.

We kissed, hugged, and said our goodbyes. I went through security and got to the gate just in time to get straight onto the plane.

As the captain began speaking over the intercom, I drifted off into a deep sleep.

Stalked

13

Back at the office, I was jetlagged, and my body was aching and cramping from sitting on the plane. It was Monday and I once again had a million voicemails, two-million emails, and a desk full of paperwork to review.

I rested my head on my desk for a moment, then pressed the intercom button to Blake's office. "Blake, would you bring me some coffee?" I murmured.

A few moments later, there was a light tap at the door. I motioned for Blake to come in, and he set the coffee on my desk and walked out without saying a word. The staff knew not to bother me for a few days after I'd returned from a trip. They all resorted to email because I was crabby and usually swamped with work.

Two hours into responding to emails, I saw another one from Anthony. I deleted it without opening it. Seeing his name threw off my energy, so I left and headed out for an early lunch.

Taking my seat in the restaurant, I pulled out my phone so I could knock out some of the voicemails. There were a few from family, all who were just checking to make sure I had made it back to New York safe and sound. I texted everyone back that I was fine.

As I put the phone down to focus on lunch, a call came in. It was from Vergil. I answered with a smile on my face, happy to hear his voice after an eventful weekend.

"Hello," I said.

"Hey, beautiful, how are you doing? How was your trip to the Lou?" he said with a friendly laugh.

"It was quite relaxing, I must say. There were a few things that went down, but we'll just leave them where they belong."

"Oh, what happened, if you don't mind me asking?" he replied.

"Just some family drama is all. I'm pretty sure most families experience drama at some point and time. I'd rather not relive it by talking about it. How was your flight back to Atlanta? We didn't get much of a chance to talk after you got back," I said.

"No worries. The flight was uneventful. I'm back to my late hours in the emergency room, not enough rest, and some lonely nights"

"Sorry to hear that, Vergil. It sounds like you're overworking."

"I need some R&R, for sure," he sighed. "I wanted to tell you I'm due to come back your way next week, to tie up some loose ends with Larry about the new clinic. I was wondering if you'd like to grab dinner after I'm settled in."

"Sure. That would be great!" I said, delighted at the prospect of seeing Vergil again.

We ended our call, and I headed back to my office. There was a bouquet of roses and another email from Anthony. I opened it. He was asking me to confirm that I had gotten the flowers. I deleted the email and threw away the flowers without even reading the note. As I did so, the door to my office swung open, and there stood Blake, barely able to contain himself with excitement.

"What in the world?" I asked.

"Boss lady, I am so sorry to barge in here like this, but I have some *GREAT* news!"

The smile on Blake's face was so wide he was starting to look like the joker from the Batman movies.

"Okay, what's going on? Spill the beans already," I said.

"We have confirmed three interviews for this issue. So far Smooth P—you know he's huge, Elle Garner, and Miss E."

"Oh my gosh, I can't believe it!"

This was our fourth issue, but the first time that we'd have celebrities in our building, in our presence, and featured in our magazine! That was surely a big deal on all levels. I couldn't believe that my childhood dream of running a successful magazine was now going to be solidified with us having celebrity guest features. The feeling was surreal. I just wished I had someone to run home to, to share the good news with . . . my own man.

When I arrived at my door that evening, I found an envelope there. I looked around to make sure no one had followed me up to my unit.

I unlocked the door, threw all my belongings on the table, and opened the envelope. It was a five-page letter from Anthony. I mean, would the man never quit? I read the letter, and it was marked "letter number one." Anthony knew that *The Notebook* was one of my all-time favorite love stories, and it looked like he was trying to use that to his advantage. He stated in the letter that he'd write me three-hundred-sixty-five letters until I came back to him or at least until I responded to his emails.

I felt so disgusted that I ripped up the letter, grabbed my cell, and called Katrina. The phone rang, but there was no answer. I paced my apartment thinking of what to do. I didn't know if this guy was psycho or what, but his behavior was starting to feel like stalking. It was making my skin crawl.

I opened my laptop and looked up an emergency number.

"This is the emergency hotline. How may I help you?" the operator said.

"I just have a quick question. If I wanted to file a restraining order against someone, what would I need to do?" I asked.

There was a slight pause, and then she said, "Ma'am, has this person you want the restraining order against caused you bodily harm on injury?"

"No, I've just been receiving endless emails, flowers, and now letters on my door."

"Ma'am, this is what you need to do. Please print out all emails and save all letters. Go to your local police station and file a report so the police have this guy on file. In the event something does happen, an immediate warrant for his arrest could then be issued."

"Well, what about getting a restraining order?" I said.

"Unfortunately, if all he's done so far is what you say, it's not enough to warrant a restraining order. That's why you need to log what happens, in case any real trouble develops. Is there anything else I can help you with this evening?"

I said no and ended the call. I rang Katrina again. "Hey, girlie, what's going on?" she said when she picked up.

"It's about Anthony."

"Oh my God, did something bad happen to him?"

"No, he's just doing some really creepy things. He won't stop sending me stuff," I said. "It feels like harassment. He says he's going to write me a letter every day until I let him see me."

"Oh, hell no, that's some creepy shit. Well, what are you going to do?" Katrina said. "I'm so glad you called me, but now you have me worried."

"Well, I've already called the emergency hotline. They said I can't get a restraining order because what he's doing isn't bad enough."

"What does that mean *isn't bad enough*? This guy could be some crazy psycho murderer, and they're just passing it off like it's not important? Monica, I'm very worried about you. Do you need me to come and stay with you tonight?"

Although some laughs, wine, and girl time would have been great, I didn't feel up to it. Plus Katrina was married and lived on the far side of the city. I felt like she needed to be at home with her family. "No, girl, that's okay," I said. "I'll be fine."

"Well, if you need anything, you make sure you let me know. Check in with me from time to time, okay?"

"Yes, I've gotcha. Don't sweat it. I'm pretty sure he's just sulking and acting like how most guys act when they've lost something great," I said.

We both laughed and ended the call. I walked into the kitchen and put on a pot of tea. While waiting for the water to boil, I bounced onto my couch and took a deep breath. Listening to the trains passing and the wind blowing outside, I fell into a daydream. I shook myself out of it when I heard the whistle coming from my teapot.

I ran to the kitchen, and the phone rang. By the time I got back to answer, no one was there. I stayed up a few more hours, reading and writing.

Reflections in the Midnight Hour

Crazy thoughts were pacing, and my heart was pounding.

The sound of trains and brisk winds against my window pane

All sounds that left me sane and feeling astounded

The light sway of the steam streaming from my teapot left calm over my room.

On a chilly dark night like tonight I was praying for my groom.

And in the mist of the midnight hour, something evil seemed lurking nearby

A feeling of disconnect, That brisk cold air out there leaving my pores dry

A shadowy face haunting the midnight hour

Lingering and smiling, setting my soul on fire.

Then I awoke with an overwhelming feeling

Like I was held down and trapped

But by who or what, I didn't know.

After moments of catching my breath

I still could feel the cold draft

And then came the rattle of another train passing by.

I was so paranoid about Anthony's behavior that I didn't know what to do with myself. I lay down and drifted off to sleep.

Mr. Doctor Business Owner

14

It was Tuesday, and I was back at the office. We were fast approaching the first set of deadlines for the next issue, so I expected Blake to come crashing into my office at any moment. The stories on my computer waiting for me to edit were minimal, the voicemail was light, and my calendar had more free space than I had seen in months. This worried me . . . but left me smiling, knowing I'd possibly get some time to myself. It was reassuring knowing we were making great time and that I was getting the hang of running a business.

I began to check my emails. There were more messages from Anthony. Based on what the emergency hotline had mentioned about needing proof of harassment, I had created a folder to dump all of his emails in.

I hit "save" and sifted through the rest of my messages. I still couldn't believe we'd have so many famous highlights for this issue and I was delighted to finally be adding the section about foster children awareness. I believed that remembering where I came from and honoring that was a noble thing.

I started in on my editing. There was more to do than I realized.

The office phone rang. It was Vergil. I was so happy at the sight of his name on the ID that my heart dropped to my stomach and warmth came over my body. I started to answer on the first ring but I waited for a few more to pass so that I could calm my excitement.

"Hey lady! How are things at the magazine?" he asked.

"Great things are happening." I told him about the celebrity interviews, and he congratulated me.

"So I'll be back out your way this weekend," he reminded me. We're still on for our date, right?"

"Of course. I wouldn't miss it for the world," I said, stammering.

I couldn't believe how awkward I felt and how absolutely ridiculous I must have been sounding to Vergil. It was just that this was the first time in a long time a man was making me weak. I hadn't felt butterflies in my stomach since I was fifteen! Anything after that and up until this point, was pretty much lust. This was the first time I really felt like a man was speaking to the queen in me. Vergil was intelligent, and he respected me as a successful woman. Vergil was the legit man I needed to complement me. One that had his own career and personality and was strong enough to help piece together the missing pieces of my puzzle of love.

"All right. I just wanted to make sure you weren't going to try to stand me up or anything," he laughed.

"No, I will so be there," I said.

As we ended our call, Blake was at the office door. The quiet of the day had finally come to an abrupt end.

"Hey, Blake, how's it going?" I asked.

"Just swimmingly. Smooth P is coming over at 3:00, so maybe you can sit in on his interview."

"That would be great. Will you knock on my door when you guys are ready to go? I want to see if I can get some of these stories edited before day's end."

The hours rolled along, and I finished my editing. I checked my emails again to see if anything important had come up. Another message from Anthony popped into my inbox. I started to delete it but opened it and read:

> *My Dearest Monica,*
>
> *Look, I know what happened between us was real. I mean, what I did was unacceptable, and I don't know how many times I'll have to apologize to you before I can get you to understand what I feel for you. Remember we were supposed to be having camp-outs by the fire, late-night walks by the bay, laughs and wine til we couldn't drink anymore? I would just REALLY appreciate it if you'd respond to me. That's all I ask.*
>
> *Anthony*

Even though the letters from Anthony seemed to be sincere, it just felt off. I had only gone on a couple of dates with the guy, and he was acting like we had been dating for years and like he couldn't go on if he couldn't have me. The guy had to be delusional! I mean, I know I'm one in a million, but come on . . . with his job and his looks, it couldn't be that hard to just move on and forget all about me.

As I closed my laptop, there was a knock at my door. It was Smooth P himself.

"You must be Ms. Walker," he said, grinning and extending his hand. "I'm Smooth P. I just wanted to come in here personally and let you know I'm honored to be supporting your success. I heard you guys were looking to raise awareness about foster youth and everything that goes along with that. I want to be the first to make sure your campaign for these kids is a success, so here is a check for $50,000. You guys can just put this away until you come together and see how you want to disburse it."

I couldn't believe it. I almost fell out of my chair when he handed me the check.

"Thank you so much. This means a lot to me as well as to my team. I'm happy to know that you want to support such a great cause," I said.

Smooth P shook my hand again, and we headed into the next room for his interview. I sat through most of it but got distracted by a text that came into my phone. It was from Anthony. I clicked delete without reading it, headed back to my office to grab my things, and exited the building for the day.

The drive home was quiet, but my mind was filling up with tension. I was kind of scared at this point. I didn't know what was going on with Anthony, and I couldn't tell what he was up to.

I was beginning to believe I was in some sort of danger. *"Maybe I'm over-thinking the situation,"* I said to myself. I didn't know if I was unsafe or if he just felt so guilty about what he had done that he couldn't move past it.

The next few days flew by! It was meeting after meeting and crunch time for the release of the magazine. I was so excited and happy with my team that I decided to present them with a surprise.

It was now Friday, and most people were still in the office. I called everyone to the conference room so that I could share the good news.

"Hey, everyone. I want to start out by saying that you guys are a fantastic, talented team, and I'm so fortunate to be working with you all. We've completed all celebrity interviews and are down to the last stretch before publication. Any problems with any teams, or are we all on target? " I asked.

Not one hand went up.

"Okay. So second order of business. I'm so excited about the success of our magazine that I want to reward every one of you with two days of extra vacation before the year is out. You can take those days whenever you'd like. Just make sure you get with your department heads so it's documented properly. Also, we all know Smooth P was in here the other day, right?"

Everyone nodded, and there was some light whispering around the room.

"Smooth P was so enthused about us adding the section and branching into the foster care arena, that he wrote us a $50,000 check just to make sure that we follow through on those efforts."

As I made the announcement, the staff went wild. I could barely hear myself think for all the chatter and applause. I silently thanked God for how beautifully the magazine was going. My success was at an all-time high.

Blake got up to make his last announcements, I stood up to leave, and Victoria followed me out of the room.

"Monica, I just want to thank you so much for everything that you do. You just don't know how many lives you will touch. For that, I thank you again," she said.

"Well, Victoria, never forget: it all was your own brilliant idea." Victoria beamed with pride, and I gave her a hug.

Vergil's plane was coming in, and I had offered to pick him up. Mr. Doctor Business Man said he had a few things he wanted to discuss with me, and I was all ears. I hit the highway and headed to the airport.

When I arrived, he was curbside, looking fine as wine, smiling like he belonged in one of my magazines. As he walked closer to the car, we made eye contact, and he asked if I would pop open the trunk.

I did, then I got out of the car to greet him with a hug. His big strong arms closed around my waist. Our cheeks met, and he lifted me from the ground, landing kisses on both sides of my face.

"I could get used to this," he said, when he put me down.

"Used to what?"

"Used to coming home to something as special as you."

"Boy, please. Close my trunk," I said, hiding a smile.

We laughed, and Vergil winked at me as he took the seat on the passenger side. His eyes twinkled with good humor. The guy sure was a charmer. I could hardly believe this was the nice but nerdy guy I remembered from college. The man had certainly learned how to impress a woman.

As I drove, Vergil directed me to Larry's place, where he would be staying. Larry lived close to the suburbs, so he was freer of the craziness I experienced living in the city. The further we drove, the bigger the houses got. The streets were tree-lined and quiet. The neighborhoods reeked of money, high status, and snooty behavior.

Vergil asked how work was, and I chatted on about the celebrity interviews and the wonderful donation Smooth P had given us. I asked Vergil how his business was going, and he looked at me with dismay in his eyes.

"Okay. We're getting there." I was surprised to see his discouragement. "Starting a business is really hard work, as I'm sure you know with your magazine," he added, trying to put the spotlight back on me. "What makes you so successful, Monica?"

"The same thing that's making you successful, Vergil," I answered, hoping to bolster his spirits. "Dedication, hard-ass work, sacrifice. There are times when it's discouraging, but a person can make it happen if they want it bad enough."

Vergil turned in his seat and looked at me. "You know, you are a really amazing woman. You've got such drive and passion for what you do. You're such an inspirational and compelling person. You really do speak to the king in me." He said this in all seriousness, then laughed, as if to hide an intensity of emotion he hadn't meant to reveal.

As we pulled up to Larry's mini-mansion, Vergil put his hand under my chin and placed a kiss on my lips. We pulled away from one another for a slight second and then went at it again.

Vergil lips were so soft, and he was a great kisser. We pulled away once more, without words, but we spoke to each other through our glances. I felt sincerity, trust, happiness . . . I saw all of those possibilities in Vergil's eyes.

When we got to Larry's front door, he was there to greet us. "Nice to see you again, Monica," he said, inviting us in.

I barely remembered Larry. He had been one of Vergil's friends when we were in college, but I smiled and said, "Nice to see you again, too. "

"I have some lemonade in the back if y'all are interested."

We chatted politely for a few seconds, then Larry grabbed Vergil by the shoulder and said he needed to speak to him for a moment. They went into the next room, while I took a seat on the beautiful white couch. I didn't mean to eavesdrop, but the house had a kind of echo, and I couldn't help hearing what Larry said.

"Hey, man. You remember what we talked about, right? Do what you have to do to seal the deal. Okay?

I had no idea what those words meant, but they were spoken in urgent tones that sounded almost conspiratorial. I felt a twinge of anxiety. Just then the guys stepped into the room again, big smiles on their faces. Vergil gave me that adorable wink again, and I melted, forgetting all about the uncomfortable feeling Larry's words had just given me.

We sat around and talked for a bit, then the conversation turned to business. Larry pulled out a blueprint of the building they were buying that would be transformed into their clinic. The guys talked shop for a while, and I decided it was time for me to leave.

"Excuse me, guys. I have to get going."

"So soon? You just got here," Larry said.

"Well, you've got a lot to talk about, and I've got a lot to get done tonight," I said.

Vergil escorted me to the door.

"Thank you so much for picking me up today and driving me over here. I'll call you later, and we'll make plans for tomorrow night," he said.

I smiled, we kissed, and I drove home. On the way, I had a funny feeling in my stomach. I kept replaying what Larry had said about "sealing the deal" in that sneaking tone of voice. It sounded like a rather crass way for two doctors to talk, even if it was business. I figured I was being silly and decided to forget about it.

When I got back to my apartment, I kept looking over my shoulder making sure that no one had followed me in. I arrived at my door, and there was a bottle of wine, a large brown envelope, and another letter from Anthony. I looked around once more, but the hallway was empty. I entered my apartment.

I dropped all of my things, threw the letter on the stack of letters from previous weeks, and sat down to open the brown envelope. In it were photographs: of me in my office, me leaving the office, me leaving my apartment, and one of Vergil and me kissing.

I dropped the photos and ran for the phone. I remembered Anthony mentioning something about being in the military, so maybe something happened that had caused him to go looney. What the heck was going on?

Sweet Lies and Poetry Rhymes

15

My heart was pounding, and my thoughts were running around like crazy. I dialed Katrina's landline, but there was no answer. Then I remembered she'd flown to Atlanta for the weekend, and was probably with Ashley and Stephanie this very moment. I was overdue for a chat with those two, so I dialed Stephanie. Sure enough. Katrina was there, with Ashley. They all got on speaker phone.

"So how is the dating thing going?" Ashly asked. "Are you writing those feelings out, girl? Come on, express yourself selflessly . . . sexually."

"Ashley, your husband must not know what to do with your ass," I said. "You are wild! Why every time you talk it gotta be sexual?"

"What in the world is going on, girl?" said Stephanie. "We haven't had a three-way call in a while, so someone has got to have some hot juicy gossip. Monica, is it you? Girl, please tell us what's happening."

As all the girls listened in, I begin to tell them my woes. "It's really good to hear y'all," I began, "except Katrina. I literally speak with her on a daily. So ya'll remember that big-time sales executive, Anthony? We went on a couple of dates, and it didn't work out because I caught him bangin' his secretary. *IN HIS OFFICE!*

"Girl Shut up! No the hell he didn't," Ashley said, unable to believe her ears.

"Was he smoking on some keisha?" Stephanie asked.

"*WHERE* the hell they do that at?" Ashley said.

"I know, we all thought he was going to be the one, right? No, turns out, I think he crazy, ya'll. So I cut him off cold-turkey. Ever since, he's emailing, writing letters, and sticking them outside my door. Now the last thing, just tonight—this dude left a bottle of wine, a letter, and an envelope full of pictures. The pictures were of me out with another guy, me coming out of my apartment, my office . . . ya'll, I'm getting scared."

The girls were gasping in disbelief on the other end of the line.

"Do we need to make a trip up there to be with you?" said Stephanie, after a minute. "'Cause girl, you know I'll be on the first flight out. All you have to do is give me the go."

"I should be fine. I called an emergency line to see if I could get a restraining order against him, and they said I had to have substantial evidence that he is a threat, or he would have to physically harm me."

"Wait a minute, Monica," said Ashley. "You mean to tell me you have to be found cut out in small pieces and buried in someone's desert before the police make a move on this guy? That is foul. I can't believe that. Monica, we are really worried about you, and if you need one of us to come and stay with you until this thing blows over, then we can do that."

I took a deep breath and sat back in my chair. I really didn't know what I wanted to do at that point. It wasn't like the guy was physically harming me; he was just being a little stalker-ish.

"Monica, you can't take something like this lightly," Katrina said. "Now you know that the guy is clearly watching you and following you. You need to put a report in tonight and fax over all of those letters from him. Forward all of the emails that he's been sending you, too. You also need to tell the police that he left photos at your doorstep, which would prove that he's been following you. What is he, a damn detective now? I know this is hard for you, girl, but we just want to make sure you are safe up there. You don't know anything about this guy and what he's capable of."

"Please, just do it for us," said Stephanie. "It's just a little piece of paper. What the hell is that going to do *IF* he actually shows up some place? But you do it, Monica. At least it's some protection if you have everything already documented with the cops."

I was taking in everything the girls were telling me, and I was kind of scared. I just didn't want to panic because they were already doing plenty of that for me. I just couldn't fathom how the poetry, anticipation, and attraction that had been my relationship with Anthony had turned into deceit, fear, and disgust.

"Sweet lies and poetry rhymes," Ashley said.

"Yeah, that guy fooled you and had you falling for the okie-doke," Katrina said.

"Well, you know that's how crazy people are!" I said. "I mean I'm no shrink, but they know how to turn that insanity on and off. Right? It's weird how that process works, and it makes me nervous because it wasn't like I knew the guy for that long. He's sending letters and stuff now, but who knows what the heck he's going to do next? You guys don't have to worry about me. My guy Vergil is in town, so I think I'm going to ask him if he can just stay with me tonight."

The girls sighed with relief once they heard I could possibly get someone to stay over. I was still upset. I was irritated and frustrated with the behavior that Anthony was displaying. It was completely juvenile.

"Okay, girlie, well we're glad to hear that," Katrina said. "Please make sure you let us know what's going on. You know we are all worried about you. I would definitely file that complaint tonight and get Vergil over there, because you know it's getting late."

"All right, ya'll," I said. "Well, thanks for the support, and I'll definitely keep you guys up to speed. I'm sure it's nothing. If I ignore him long enough, hopefully he'll get the message and just leave me the heck alone."

We all laughed, shared our love for one another, and ended the call.

I sat at the table for a while thumbing through the letters that Anthony had left at my door. I just didn't understand where all of this was coming from. They were five and six pages long, and I just didn't get how you could have so much on your mind like that for a person you barely knew.

This had convinced me that Anthony was both crazy and that he was carrying some serious baggage from a previous relationship; he had carried that mess over to me. He did tell me his ex moved to Colorado, leaving him behind, I remembered. Maybe she moved because he was completely insane in the damn membrane.

Later that night, I called the emergency hotline back. Apparently the photos Anthony had taken of me constituted enough of a threat for them to not just blow me off again. The lady on the line said I qualified for a restraining order now, and Anthony would not be allowed to come near my car, residence, or place of employment. He couldn't even approach me in the grocery store.

Those words coming out of her mouth gave me a strong sense of reassurance. But I still didn't want to stay at home alone that night. And the restraining order couldn't be issued until the police station offices opened in the morning.

I called Vergil.

"Hey, honey. It's getting pretty late. How's everything going?" he asked. I could hear the smile in his voice.

"Not too good. I've got a problem, and I don't feel safe. I didn't want to involve you in this . . . There's this guy I dated. Now he's scaring me. Do you think you could come and sleep on my couch tonight? I'm sorry to ask . . . "

"Look, sweetie, if you are afraid, I'm going to be there for you, no questions asked. I care deeply for you, Monica, and I wouldn't dare allow anything to happen to you. Do you need me to bring anything? And what's wrong, did something serious happen? Is that why you're so afraid?"

"Yes, something did happen. Can you come now and I'll give you the details later?"

"Just hold tight and I'll be there in thirty minutes," he said. "I'll call a cab."

After I hung up the phone, I snuggled under a quilt on the couch for a while. I guess I fell asleep, because I awoke to a knock at the door.

I jumped up and looked around to make sure I was still inside alone. I grabbed the baseball bat I kept next to my fireplace and approached the peephole with it.

"Who is it?" I muttered.

By this time it was about one in the morning, and I could hear the trains passing, the shuffling of street rats, and the 'woosh' sound that a car makes when it speeds by.

It was Vergil, thank the Lord.

As I opened the door, I breathed in the aroma of his cologne and greeted him with a hug. He smelled of Lever 2000, and his skin rubbing against my face was smooth.

"My goodness, baby, are you okay? I brought you some wine and this rose. Thought you might like that."

"Why, thank you. That was very sweet."

We sat down on the couch, and Vergil poured us two glasses of the wine. I told him the story of Anthony, right up to the latest episode, and about the restraining order they said I could get in the morning.

"Monica baby, this guy is nuts,' Vergil said, shaking his head. "If you need me to stay for a few nights, I'm happy to. I'll sleep on the couch, of course. I just want to make sure you're okay."

He placed his hand on my cheek. I closed my eyes and shifted in my seat. He then kissed my forehead and both of my cheeks, then my lips.

"I'd better get you some linens and a towel," I said, not wanting things to go too far. Kissing Vergil felt fantastic, but I was determined to stick to my standards this time and not jump into bed with the guy. I was going to clean up my ways and stay celibate til I got married.

Vergil got up, looked out the windows, checked the front door, and placed the bat next to the couch. I brought him a pillow and blanket and tucked a sheet around the seat cushions.

"If you need anything, I'll be right here, babe."

"Okay," I said, gratefully.

Vergil watched me as I shuffled out of the living room. I got into bed and underneath the covers. I fell right asleep, feeling safe and protected.

The next morning I awoke early to muffled sounds in the kitchen. I flipped over to see what time it was. Five-thirty! I didn't have to be into the office until ten that day, but apparently Vergil had to leave earlier and was trying to quietly make breakfast.

"Good morning, sleepyhead," he said when I shuffled into the kitchen. "Did you have a good night?"

"Slept like a baby," I said with a giggle. I felt happy—so different than the night before. Here was a man who cared about me enough to come over at the drop of a hat when I needed him—and now, it appeared, the man could even cook!

Vergil leaned down and kissed me on the forehead, and I smacked his derriere as I left the kitchen. "I'm going to shower," I called over my shoulder, "and then we can enjoy that breakfast."

"Sounds great to me," he called back. "Take your time."

I brushed my teeth and stepped into the shower. Making sure the water wasn't too hot, I allowed the warm steam to wet my body. I stepped under the nozzle and surrendered myself to the warmth. I took a deep breath and let out a sigh of relief. With Vergil nearby, I felt safe again. It seemed like all my dreams were finally coming true. .

I twirled underneath the spray with closed eyes and a sense freedom. My mind was clear, and at that moment, I didn't have a care in the world. I lathered, rinsed, and wrapped a big towel around my torso. I liked to do that rather than rub myself dry.

I tiptoed into the kitchen and playfully muttered, "Boo!"

Vergil jumped a mile and whirled to face me. He shoved a drawer closed that he had been rummaging in.

"Woman, don't sneak up on me like that!" he said, irritation in his voice.

"Sorry. Didn't mean to startle you," I said. I hoped I hadn't spoiled the good mood of the morning. "What are you looking for?" I asked.

Vergil went back to the stove and began dishing up bacon and eggs. "Just looking for the silverware," he mumbled.

"I keep that in this drawer," I said, removing two sets of forks and knives and putting them on the table. "You sure have got it smelling good in here."

"Yeah, I can cook breakfast, but that's about it," he said.

I went over to hug him, but he seemed a little jittery and uneasy.

"Is everything okay?" I said. "You seem a little off. Are you upset with me because I said 'boo'?"

"No, babe. I just didn't sleep too well last night," he answered.

"Oh, no. I'm so sorry. You don't have to stay over again if the couch feels uncomfortable. I have a friend who can come stay with me for a few days if that's going to be easier for you. Look, I know this is a lot to just throw at someone.

Especially with us just linking back up after all these years. I just didn't know who else to call," I said.

Vergil put his hand under my chin and looked at me with those soft, dreamy eyes. "Look, Monica, don't go beating yourself up over this. No one deserves to go through what you're going through, and they definitely don't deserve to do it alone. I'm a man; I'm supposed to protect you. Don't worry. Now let's eat before the food gets cold, okay baby?"

With that, he tenderly kissed my cheek. I smiled, and we sat down to say grace over the food. After we'd eaten, Vergil wished me a good day and headed out to meet Larry. I assumed they'd be getting some more stuff done for setting up their clinic.

I got up from the table and cleared the kitchen. I noticed the drawer Vergil had been rummaging in was still partly open. I pulled it out and looked inside. He had been looking in the drawer where I keep my important papers.

The realization made me suddenly feel chilled. *Don't be silly,* I scolded myself. *He was just looking for the silverware drawer.* This Anthony business was making me paranoid. I didn't want to turn into one of those cynical women who distrusted all men because she'd had a couple of bad experiences.

I threw on my clothes and headed for the police station. The sun was shining, birds were singing, and it was going to be a gorgeous day. I knew I was going to feel right as rain once I had that restraining order in place. And Vergil had just texted that he was taking me out to dinner tonight. I felt like skipping up the sidewalk, like a schoolgirl.

A Knock on the Door

16

Several weeks went by, and there had been no more contact from Anthony. It was like he had disappeared off the face of the planet. Apparently the restraining order had done the trick.

Vergil and I continued to date on the weekends when he could fly up, and things were as saucy as ever. He planned to move to New York soon, and I could hardly wait.

One morning I woke up, opened the morning newspaper outside my front door, and saw my magazine featured on the front page. I jumped up and down, squealing like a kid in a candy shop. I trampled over everything in my way trying to make it to my purse for my phone.

I rang Blake. It sounded like I had woken him up.

"Blake, you won't believe this! We're going to the moon, baby! I just picked up this morning's news, and our magazine is featured on the front page!"

"Shut the front door! You can't be serious," he answered, now fully awake.

A reporter had been by the office and interviewed some staff members and me a couple of weeks back, so we knew we were getting some sort of coverage, but seeing the magazine featured on Page One of the city's most popular paper came as a total shock.

"No, this is the God-honest truth," I said, tossing myself down on the sofa. I read Blake the first few paragraphs.

"I can't believe it. This will put the magazine front and center into the city's awareness. We couldn't buy that sort of publicity, not for a million bucks. It's a dream come true," he said.

I moved to the kitchen and grabbed my cup of coffee, spilling some of its contents.

"That's for sure," I answered. "New York is a beast, so who could know what they were going to write about us? But they like us, Blake. They *love* us. And their mention of the foster kids awareness campaign ought to bring in lots of donations."

"All I can say is, 'wow,'" said Blake—for once at a loss for words.

"Thank you so much, Blake," I said. "None of this stuff would be happening if it weren't for you and my fabulous team."

"Well, thank you, Ms. Monica. But the credit is all yours. And I couldn't have asked for a better boss."

As we ended the call, I glanced over the paper one last time in disbelief. I placed it on the table in front of me and thought, *I need to get this laminated. This is a great accomplishment.*

I got on the phone and called all my family, Vergil, and close friends. They were thrilled for my success. Of course my mom told me that she knew I could do it.

I hung the phone on the charger and prepped myself for the gym. When I got there, several people glanced over at me with smiles, and a few called, "Congratulations on the article!" as they walked by. They'd recognized my face from the paper.

I felt like an overnight celebrity. I just wished Vergil was in town, so he could celebrate with me. I'd have to wait until Monday to celebrate with my staff. I was going to take them all out to lunch and give them the afternoon off.

After I was done working out, I headed home to shower. When I got near my apartment, I did what I always did: look down the hall to make sure no one had followed me.

But when I got to the door, there was another letter. My heart jumped into my throat as I struggled to find my key.

When I got inside, I closed and locked the door, starring at it a few seconds. I slowly backed up until the back of my knees touched the couch. I flopped down on the couch and slowly opened the letter.

> *My dearest Monica,*
>
> *Look, I don't know what sort of game you are trying to play with me, but the love that I have for you is real. You're the last thing I can think about at night and the first thing that comes to mind every morning. I think about you on the train when I'm going to work, when I visit the Italian restaurant and pizza joints . . . I can't get you out of my head. It's like you're a part of me. I know you think I'm crazy, but when you're in love, it makes you do some crazy things.*
>
> *I've even blacked out a few times. I just don't understand why you are refusing to communicate with me. Am I really not human? Am I not a man? Am I not*

allowed to make mistakes as a man? You have to forgive me. I never meant to hurt you, and I promise the next time I will be a better man. You have opened my eyes, Monica. I was blind, but now I see. You are a phenomenal woman who was cut from a very rare piece of cloth. You have your own brains, beauty . . . and I see that now. That secretary didn't mean anything to me, and that was before I knew you. That was before I knew that I would and could feel this way about someone. I feel lost without you. I feel like a piece of me is missing, like I can't live, sleep, or breathe without you. Monica, please respond to me, will you do that? I can't go on without you, and if I can't have you, I don't know what I'll do. Anthony

Tears invaded my eyes as I read over the last sentence. I called family, my home girls, the police. Last, I called Vergil.

"Vergil, are you there?" I asked when he picked up.

"Yes, baby what's wrong? Why are you crying? I thought you were happy today."

I had completely forgotten about our earlier phone call, and the happiness I'd felt about the newspaper article. That seemed so far away now, like it had happened a hundred years ago, or to someone else, not me.

"I'm flying out there, babe," Vergil said, sounding really concerned. "And you need to call the police."

"I already did. I don't want you making a trip out here just for me."

"I need to come up and take care of business, anyway, so don't you worry about it, Monica. I'll be there in a few hours. Keep the door locked til I get there, okay?"

"Okay," I said.

After that, I cried a while and fell asleep on the couch. I awoke to a completely dark apartment and a tapping noise. I jumped up and looked through the spyhole in my front door. No one was there.

A text came through on my phone. It was Anthony. There was a knock. I froze. I looked through the peephole again. Anthony's face was there, up close to the hole, leering back at me.

"Go away!" I yelled.

I dialed the police. They didn't pick up.

"Baby, just let me in. I want to speak with you," he said.

"What do you want from me? It's over, and there's nothing to discuss. Just go away and leave me the hell alone," I said.

I flipped on the light and ran to grab the baseball bat from beside the fireplace. The police line finally answered. I told them there was a stalker outside my door. They took down my address. "Please hurry!" I whispered into the phone. "I'm afraid he might kick his way in!"

Another texted chimed into my phone, and it was from him.

My cell phone rang—also him. Tears trickled down the side of my face. I pressed the ignore button, but still he called—twenty more times to be exact. When I didn't answer, another text message came in. Anthony was expressing how very angry he was getting—more and more every second I allowed him to wait outside. A big bang came over my door.

"Let me the hell in! I don't know why you are treating me like this. I am madly in love with you, and if I can't have you, no one else ever will!"

There was a commotion outside the door. It sounded like another guy had intervened. I peered through the spyhole, and Vergil was there. I flung open the door, and the two men stumbled into my apartment. Vergil landed a slug to the right side of Anthony's face. The force caused Anthony to fall back onto the sofa.

The old lady that lived across the hall opened her door. She shook her head and slowly closed it again. Anthony stood up and landed a blow on Vergil. The two fought for several minutes, and then the police arrived. They pulled the men apart and apprehended them both.

"No, this one didn't do anything," I pleaded. "He was defending me." I told them about the restraining order, and showed them my copy of it.

The police released Vergil and took Anthony away. I hugged Vergil liked I'd never hugged a man before. He was my true hero; he had saved me from a night that could have ended a lot differently.

"Thank you so much, babe," I cooed. "I've never had anyone just come to my rescue like that."

"That's what I'm here for," he said. "You never have to worry about that guy ever again." He smiled and added, "I have something to tell you." He pulled me to the couch. We sat down, and he took both my hands and gazed into my eyes.

"Baby, I'm moving to the city. Now—not in a several months, as I had planned. Larry has agreed to let me stay at his place, so I'm here for good, baby. What do you think of that?"

"Vergil! That's fantastic!" I yelled.

I jumped into his arms, kissed him, and wrapped my arms around his neck. I closed my eyes and inhaled the scent of his cologne. I wrapped one hand around the back of his head, caressing his face with the other. He closed his eyes and let out a deep sigh.

Then we started kissing. We opened our mouths, and our tongues intertwined. Vergil stood up, and I wrapped my legs around his waist. He walked me into the bedroom, undressing me with one hand as he held me up with the other.

I felt safe, I felt loved, and I felt like Vergil was about to put it on me like none other. He laid me across the bed, and I reached up and took off his shirt. All my intentions about not having sex before marriage were forgotten. We made fast, passionate love, as if we had been starving for each other.

Afterwards, our bodies fell limp against the mattress. Our racing breaths became light sighs.

The realization crashed into my awareness: I had broken one of my rules: remaining celibate until the man had committed to me.

Vergil picked me up and carried me to the shower.

The next morning I woke up with a pounding headache. I felt around on the other side of my bed to see if Vergil was there. He was gone. He'd left a glass of orange juice, breakfast, a rose, and note on the night stand. I looked over at the items, bounced the back of my head into my pillow, closed my eyes and smiled, letting out a deep sigh.

I flung the covers off of my body and headed for the bathroom.

I looked into the mirror and asked myself if what really went down the night before was real. I felt like I had awakened this morning from a terrible nightmare.

I walked into the living room. From the way the place looked, I knew that Anthony coming after me had been no dream. My wooden bat was broken in half, the glass coffee table was broken . . . my living room was in complete disarray. I could tell that Vergil must have tried to clean some of the mess up before he left, but there was still a lot to be done. I threw my head back and strolled into the kitchen, feeling like a zombie. My body was so exhausted.

I was pouring a glass of water when the phone rang. It was Stephanie. Katrina was the one usually calling to get the scoop.

"Hey, girlie, what's up?" she said. "I heard you got another letter from that stalker yesterday, and I wanted to call and make sure you were okay."

Heading into the bedroom, I pulled the covers back and rolled myself into the bed.

"Girl, you don't know the half of it," I said. "He came to the apartment last night, yelling 'fuck' and banging on my door. Scared me out of my wits! I called 911, but Vergil got here first. The cops arrested Anthony."

"Lord, I was afraid it would come to this. You did the smart thing filing that restraining order. Now the dude's in trouble big. He'd be a fool to bother you again. You okay?"

"I've got a pounding headache, but I'm not scared anymore, with Vergil here. I'm going to be okay."

"Well, something traumatizing has transpired. So you definitely need to take the proper time to heal and get yourself together." Stephanie was a clinical psychologist, so she knew exactly what to say when someone had gone through something like this. "And don't go feeling like what happened was in some silly way your fault. That guy was a complete lunatic. You're safe and sound—that's the important thing," she said.

We talked some more, but I didn't tell Stephanie I had had sex with Vergil. I was embarrassed. I had compromised on my own rules again.

"So this Vergil guy," she said. "He seems to be taking a strong liking to you. That's great, girl! I wish I had a guy that would just drop all of what he was doing to be by my side. Well, I do. You know my husband is a great man, but what Vergil did for you last night, that's very noteworthy. I think he really has a thing for you. We'll all have to meet this guy one day."

"Soon enough," I said, "but I've been thinking we all should take that girls' trip we've been talking about. At this point in time, I am in desperate need of a getaway."

Stephanie laughed through the phone and started throwing out some suggestions. "*YES*, that would be so fun," she said. "I think all of us are in need of a girls' trip. You know Katrina is the queen of planning. We should come up with a place and appoint her to plan it out. She loves that stuff."

We agreed that we'd do a three-way call later that week to plan the trip. My mood changed knowing that I'd soon be lying on some beach sipping mojitos.

Stephanie and I ended the call, and I fell back asleep. I must have slept most of the morning, when I heard a knock on the front door. It was Vergil. He had returned to help me clean up the night-before mess. He asked if I was going in to work, and I told him I needed some time off.

"Well, baby, it's beautiful outside today," he said. "No need to mope around the house. Anthony's gone, and you know I'm here to protect you. Let's go grab some food, then go do something fun. What do you say?" He gave me that winning smile.

"Okay, fine. If you insist, I'll go," I said, not particularly in the mood.

I got up, popped a couple of Tylenol, and we took the next hour cleaning the front room and rearranging furniture. "You know you looked really good sweeping like that," Vergil said, as I pushed some broken glass into a pile with a broom.

"Oh, shut up. I look a mess," I said, secretly pleased. Vergil found me beautiful even when I had a headache and must have looked like death warmed over.

In the bathroom, I turned on the shower. In the midst of gargling with mouthwash, I saw Vergil in the mirror come in and place his hands over my eyes.

"Come on, babe, quit playing. I can't see," I said.

"What's the magic word?" he asked.

"Please."

He turned me around, picked me up, and placed me on the sink. He ran his hand through my hair and told me how beautiful I was. He was completely naked and ready for more action.

"Okay, can we stop?" I said.

"What's wrong? Did I do something wrong?"

"No. It's just that I made a promise to myself a few weeks ago. I really want to save all of my goodies for marriage. I've been putting the carriage before the horse for far too long. Last night happened completely in the heat of the moment. Can we just hold off on that until the appropriate time?"

"Sure, baby," he said. "Thank you so much for telling me. I completely respect you and would never want to do anything to make you feel uncomfortable. I'll wait as long as you want me to wait. You are worth it, baby, and you deserve the best."

I smiled and kissed Vergil on his nose.

I hit the shower and got dressed. We left the apartment and headed for to the train. There was already so much traffic that neither of us felt like driving. The day was going perfectly. Vergil was so sweet. He held my hand; I stood in front of him on the train as he held me close.

After we got off, we walked a ways and ran into a carnival.

"Wow, this is amazing," I said. "I haven't been to a carnival since I was in college."

"I know, right? I came across it last night on my way to your place. It was closed, of course. Now baby, you know I'm very competitive, right? I hope you brought you're A-game with you."

"No worries," I said. "So that means I should have brought an extra bag for all the gifts you're going to win for me, right?"

Vergil leaned down and kissed me on the forehead. "Let's go get some hot dogs," he said.

As we walked to the hot dog stand, I looked around and viewed all of the other couples, smiling and having so much fun. They looked happy, and I was happy as well. I couldn't have asked for a better guy.

Throughout the day, we did everything. Played games, ate until we couldn't eat any more, and last but not least, ended our night on the Ferris wheel.

"That'll be five tickets a piece," the Ferris wheel operator said.

Vergil handed the guy ten tickets, and we closed ourselves into the little caged pumpkin-like unit. Vergil grabbed my hands and landed a passionate kiss to the left side of my face. He loved doing that.

"I had a really great time out here with you today," he murmured. "Monica, it's time you know that I am in love with you. I have loved you ever since college. I was just too much of a wuss to present myself to you. You are a great woman, and I love that you are so passionate about life and all that you do. You're smart, courageous, and you have a beautiful heart."

I was overwhelmed with happiness.

At that moment, Vergil reached into his pocket and pulled out a small blue-velvet box. I pressed my cheeks in disbelief, and tears trickled down.

"Monica Raschell Walker, will you make me the happiest man in the world and become my wife?" he asked.

For a moment, words and breath had both escaped my body.

"Yes, I will," I said.

He wrapped his arms around me and kissed me like he loved me. I held my hand out in front of me and peered at the two-karat yellow-diamond ring. It was beautiful. We had gotten engaged at the very top of the Ferris wheel. I'd remember that moment forever.

After we left the carnival, Vergil took me home and headed to Larry's house. I dropped onto the couch as I always did and looked at the rock once more. I was still in disbelief. I was getting ready to become someone's Mrs.

That night I called all of my family and friends to let them know about the engagement. Everyone was so happy for me, especially my mom and dad. I never thought the moment would come, but it had finally arrived. I felt like Monica had finally arrived.

The next day at work, everyone noticed a glow.

"Hey, Monica," Blake said. "You look amazing. Did I miss something? You look as pleased as if you won the lottery."

I popped up my left hand to show the sparkling piece I had on my finger.

"Shut the front door! *NO!* He did *not* propose to you!" Blake said.

"Yes, he did, and I cannot express enough how overjoyed and surprised I am. I mean, I never thought this moment would come, and it's finally here."

"Why not? You are an amazing woman. Hell, if I wasn't gay, I'd have flopped down on one knee and asked you my damn self. Monica, you've got it all together. You have your career, you're gorgeous … you deserve the best, and Vergil seems like a guy who'd give you the world and more."

Blake wrapped his arms around me and made the announcement to the rest of the office. A loud uproar of happiness and applause flooded the room. I yelled out a loud "thank you."

Later, I got on a three-way call with the girls to start planning the trip to Cancun. After Katrina had agreed to take full control of planning the escape, I ended the call so I could get caught up on my real work.

We were now approaching the deadline for the next issue. I started calling back people who had left me voice messages. I smiled, feeling like my old self again. The scene with Anthony seemed like it had happened ages ago. My mind was swept up in the joy of Vergil's love for me. I felt proud.

After answering the majority of the voicemails, I moved over to my emails. Apparently the reviews were so good for our last issue that more agents were contacting me about having their clients featured in our magazine. One email read:

Dear Ms. Walker:

We are looking to raise more awareness for two of our emerging artists— Jazzy K and Christine Michele—who both will be releasing albums by year's end. Is it possible for Enterprise 25 to do a feature on them? They both will be available for Skype interviews the third week of this month, and of course, we can provide you with photos. Please let us know if you are interested.

Thanks for your time and consideration.

Crooked Mile Recording

I couldn't believe what I was seeing. As long as we were getting topnotch artists to feature in our issues, we were destined to stay placed at the front of all magazine stands. I sent an email over to Veronica in PR and asked her to schedule the interviews.

Two other emails came in with youth stories we could add to the magazine's new fostering and parenting section. That section was really picking up speed. We'd decided that the $50,000 Smooth P. had given us would go to help support teens looking to graduate high school and go college. The awards would be $5,000 apiece, and each applicant would write an essay letting us know what they'd be using the funds for and why they deserved to be selected. Students that won would then be featured in the magazine.

That night after work, I went home tired, and ready to make plans for our annual girls' trip. When I phoned Katrina, she had already written out the entire itinerary for Cancun, Mexico. The total cost for the trip was about $2,000 apiece.

"Hey, girlie, you ready to go?" said Katrina. "I know you need a vacation after all the craziness that's been going on in your life."

"That's for sure. I've been waiting for this vacation all year!"

"Have you started planning the wedding?"

The wedding was the last thing on my mind. I really needed a breather. Everything was just happening too fast.

"I've begun thinking about it. I'm just taking everything a day at a time at this point. I'll worry about that after this trip and after we finish this next issue of the magazine," I said.

"I'll bet your mom is so excited."

It was true. My mom was probably more excited than I was. For like the last five years, she had pestered me about when that special day would come. I was leaving all of the planning to her. She liked that sort of thing. My mom was known for the big Thanksgiving get-together and the year-end Christmas party. She absolutely *LOVED* event planning, and I was happy because planning a wedding was definitely something I needed outside help with.

"So are we shooting for the second week in September for Cancun?" I asked. I was ready to book it and I didn't even care where, as long as it was far away from New York for a while.

"Yep, everyone's pretty much agreed on that, so we are good to go," said Katrina.

I was thinking about the magazine and how I wanted to make sure everything was in place for before I left town for an entire week.

"All right, so let's do it," I said.

Cancun

17

The next few weeks flew by, and before I could believe it, I was on my way to Cancun. I had all my sexy swimwear ready, and enough bug repellant for a week. I read that Cancun was pretty hot, so I made sure to pack a lot of breathable clothing and put my hair in braids.

That morning Vergil drove me to the airport. I'd be meeting the girls when I got to Mexico. I wasn't looking forward to four hours in the air. Taking a seat by the loading gate, I closed my eyes and took a deep breath.

Monica, everything will be fine, I told myself. *This will be a great trip and a time to get your mind together. When you come home, you'll be ready to start planning for the happiest day in your life, your wedding!*

I took my seat on the plane and turned the knob above my head so the air wasn't blowing directly on me. The flight attendant approached the center aisle and motioned all of the safety instructions. Then the captain came over the intercom. The temperature was 102 in Cancun, he said.

As we hit the runway and became airborne, I sat back and covered myself with a blanket, knowing I'd fall asleep at any moment. The cold air on the plane always made me sleepy.

Four hours passed faster than I could imagine. We were already there, and the scenery from the window, as the plane landed, was absolutely beautiful. I'd heard about the azure water and brilliant-white sand beaches, but seeing them for the first time, especially from the air, was breathtaking.

We were staying at Hotel El Ray del Caribe. When the airport van dropped me there, the girls were sitting down in the lobby, waiting for me.

"*AHHHHHHHH,*" they screamed when I walked in the door.

"Come on now, ya'll," I said. "We haven't even been here an hour and ya'll are already about to get us kicked out."

"You look so friggin' pretty, and you're absolutely glowing. Let's see the rock!" Ashley cried, grabbing my left hand.

All of the girls gasped for air as they stared at the yellow two-karat diamond. The Mexican sun was flowing in and onto the rock, making it look magical.

"Oh, girl, you better keep him. He must really love you if he's getting you ice like this. Wow, this guy has taste," Ashley said.

We grabbed our bags and headed up to our living quarters, chattering as we waited for the elevator to stop. The door opened, we entered the hall, and made a left turn.

"Wait, what room are we staying in?" Stephanie asked.

Katrina pulled out the sheet and checked. When we found the door and opened it, the views from the suite were breathtaking. The ocean stretched away as far as the eye could see—a shade of blue so pure and deep as I'd never seen before. There was a magnificent view of the pool, and the hotel architecture was to die for. The windows were open, and the Cancun heat grazed us as we walked in.

I flounced onto one of the beds and took in the beauty. We had finally arrived.

Our day of flying had all of us pretty much drained, so we all showered, had dinner in the gorgeous hotel restaurant, then sat with drinks by the pool. We were too tired to hit the bars and nightclubs that stretched out along the beach. When we returned to our suite, everyone was laughing, and Stephanie was half-drunk.

"Hey, girlie, ya' better slow down," teased Ashely. "We still have like six days to go."

Katrina grabbed the itinerary and went over what we were to expect for Day Two. "Ladies, let's settle down for a few," she said. "Looks like tomorrow we're going to meet with a tour guide, and I'll let him tell us what we'll be doing next."

All of the ladies jumped into their jammies, and we turned off like lights.

The next day we had breakfast in the lobby. The tour guide was patiently waiting for us to get done eating when he approached our table.

"Good morning, ladies. My name is Terrance, and I'll be your tour guide for today's exciting excursion," he said.

"Good morning," we giggled in unison. Terrance was cute! He had a sleek haircut and a trim little beard. His posture was upright and proper, and his Hispanic accent alluring.

"Girl, is it me or will we have something to eye for the next few hours?" Ashley whispered as Terrance turned and spoke to a bus boy passing by.

Katrina popped Ashley on the arm. "Quiet before he hears you."

"Hey, I'm an almost married woman now," I said holding up my bling.

"Today we'll be venturing off to Cancun-Merida," said Terrance, coming back to our table. He motioned toward a mini-van waiting outside the lobby door. "When you ladies are ready, we can board."

We grabbed our belongings and headed for the van. It looked quite comfortable.

"Once you are nice and comfortable in your seats, I'll explain the rest of the trip," said Terrance, as we all climbed in. "There are blankets in the back if anyone would care to have one. They keep it pretty chilly on the rides over," he smiled.

Terrance got into the front seat, and the driver walked around to close the doors behind us.

"Hey, Terrance, you know you could come and sit back here with us. You know, help keep us warm?" Stephanie flirted.

"Thanks, but where I'm sitting is just fine. If you ladies are chilly, there are plenty of blankets in the back," he repeated.

We laughed. Terrance was very professional and proper, and I liked that about him. I wasn't the only one who had noticed how tasty he was, but I had a nice tall glass of chocolate milk waiting for me on my return home, so I was happy. I smiled, thinking of my honey. The van slowly pulled into the road.

"Now the drive is going to be about five hours," said Terrance, "so please get comfortable. We will hit a few bumps and sketchy spots, but for the most part the ride should be smooth, and the weather clear. It'll be pretty hot when we get there, so drink plenty of fluids and suck up this cool air while you can. En route we'll stop at the ruins of Chichen Itza, including the famous pyramid, Castle el Castillo. Please let me know if there's anything you may need. Thank you."

All of the ladies were so tired from jet lag that at the sound of Terrance's last word, everyone was out, including me. I awoke to an abrupt stop and the sound of the mini-van door sliding open. I turned and spotted Terrance exiting the vehicle. He was now standing in front of the van conversing with the driver.

"Hey, ya'll, I think we're here," I said.

The other girls stretched and got out of the van. The ruins in front of us were absolutely beautiful.

"Hey, anyone have any gum?" muttered Katrina. "I feel a little tart."

I reached in my purse and grabbed a pack of Altoids. The girls passed it around and began to snap pictures. I opened my camera and started snapping away as well. I had an "aha" moment. I was going to add this trip to the travel section in the magazine's next issue.

The tour guide approached us. "Hey ladies," he said. "Hope you're well-rested. So this is the beautiful pyramid of Chichen Itza. It was built by the Maya in 432 A.D. Pay attention to the structure and the details of each piece. The Mayans did not have all the technology and metric systems like architects have today. They were a very talented group of people. Here we are in the twenty-first century, and this structure still stands. Feel free to snap as many pictures as you'd like. Please just be careful where you step."

"Is anyone thirsty? Because it's as hot as Satan's ass out here," Katrina said.

After we'd walked around a while, we returned to the van to drink water and wipe our faces. The heat was sweltering, but I was enjoying every minute of the trip. For once I didn't have a care in the world.

We re-buckled up and headed down the road to our next destination. The girls were now wide awake, so conversation and laughter rang out from the van. When we stopped again, the driver opened the door for us, and we all stepped out.

"Here we are at the foot of the pyramid, Castle El Castillo," announced Terrance. "It's a ninety-one-step pyramid and one of the most visited places in the country. You ladies are free to take pictures and explore the site. Safety first, so please walk. There is also a restroom right ahead."

"Hey, Terrance, would you mind taking a picture of us all?" I asked.

The girls and I ran to the front of the pyramid steps and took a bunch of goofy and fun photos. We hung out there for a while then headed back to the van.

When we got to the hotel a little while later, the front desk clerk informed us that there was no air-conditioning in any of the units. I just knew it would be a long and uncomfortable night of sleep.

After dinner, the girls and I ventured out on our own. We tried all sorts of food and drinks and even enjoyed a festival going on not too far from the hotel.

The next morning was day three of our trip. We were getting ready to embark on another long ride, so we packed our belongings and headed to the lobby area. Everyone was pretty quiet and dragging.

"Hey, is everybody having fun?" asked Stephanie. "I know I am, but they can have this heat. It's too damn hot out here."

"That's for sure," said Katrina. "I'm having a great time, but baby, this heat is for the birds."

When we finished eating breakfast, we gathered in the common area, waiting for Terrance to let us know what the day had to offer.

"Good morning ladies. I hope you all are well today," he said. "We have the mini-van waiting out in the front. I hope you have collected all of your belongings, as we will not be returning. Please step forward and we will get going."

The girls and I entered the van, as we did several times before. Assuming that we now knew the procedures for the van, Terrance went right into what was ahead.

"Today we will be driving to explore the Palenque Ruins. There will be about two-hundred buildings which make up that ancient Mayan city. Upon our arrival, there will be another tour guide, and he'll talk about the culture, history, and the Mayans' beliefs and ceremonies. We will also climb to the top of towers to view their tropical jungle and the Yucatan Plain. Please get comfy, and we should be there shortly."

The girls and I weren't so quick to fall asleep this time around. We snapped pictures of the beautiful scenery and conversed amongst ourselves to pass the time.

"Is it just me or does anyone else miss their man as much as I do?" asked Katrina. "He gets on my damn nerves sometimes, but I could use his arms around me right about now."

"Yes, girl. I miss my Vergil honey," I said. "He's probably back in New York working like a slave."

"I meant to ask you about that, Monica. When are they opening up the clinic?" Ashley asked.

"Well, I don't have all of the logistics. I've been over to see it, and it's pretty nice. I think Larry and Vergil will operate out of the ground-floor suits and rent the top space out. I don't believe they'll want to rent to just any old body, maybe other practitioners," I said.

"Well, that's great, girl. You always had an eye for a guy that had it all together," Stephanie said.

I kind of agreed with her to a certain extent. I did have an eye and heart for a great guy who had it all together. Some of them just happened to be crazy, possessive, or just downright not good for me.

The girls and I had been talking for so long that we had chatted ourselves all the way to our destination. We'd made a few stops in between. Since there weren't a lot of gas stations, we'd had to do the old pop-a-squat trick behind some trees whenever we needed a restroom.

As we exited the van, we looked out over a small modern city built around an ancient Mayan city. The views were tropical, and the terrain smelled of fresh rain. The people were very friendly. We headed to Hotel Xibulba, as we would be staying there for the next two nights.

The second tour guide arrived and led us into the ruins of the ancient city. Our first stop was a chapel with a floor completely covered in pine needles. The girls and I thought it was strange, but it was a part of what the Mayans believed in.

We interacted with the villagers and for the next two days explored their customs, ate their food, and cooled off at one of the most beautiful waterfalls I had ever seen in my life. I felt like I was in a scene from a movie.

On days five and six we traveled to another small city and stayed at Hotel Paraden Margarita. On Day Seven we took salsa lessons, did a volcano climb, and headed to the airport to return to our respective homes.

"Ladies, I had an amazing time with you all," I said, as we parted. "So glad we got to catch up. This trip was just what I needed," I said.

"It was so good seeing you girls again," said Ashley, hugging Ashley and Stephanie, who were flying back together to Atlanta.

"We love you," said Stephanie. "Stay safe, and Monica, let us know all the whens and wheres for the wedding."

"*YES*, please do, and make sure you invite some fine tenders," Ashley added.

As the ladies walked away, I felt a little sad. Katrina and I walked to our gate and checked with the attendant to see how long it would be before the plane boarded. I had an hour left to spare, and Katrina wanted to read a magazine, so I took out my notebook.

> *Sometimes the best things in life are free. Like valuable relationships, for instance. I just had a wonderful time in Cancun, Mexico with my girls, and I wouldn't change that experience for anything in the world. Now that we are all older and have our own separate and personal lives, it's often hard to meet at a common ground and plan things such a trip. It's especially hard for me. Running a magazine, having people on a payroll and an image to uphold is enough to drive anybody insane. I love my life, though, and I love the curveballs it sometimes throws at me. I'm getting ready to marry the love of my life and embark on an entirely different path. One I've never walked down before. It is nerve-wrecking and hard to keep up with my life at times, but I know and believe I can do it. I have a pretty strong backbone. I have a loving and supportive family, supportive friends, and my magazine team. What more could a girl want? What else is there in life to want or desire?*

Newly Engaged

18

When I returned to New York, there was so much I needed to get done. I had a wedding to plan for and a magazine to run. There were bridesmaids to hurdle up, colors to be picked, and venues to be selected—a date, a time, and a place. Let me not even get started on what dress I'd be wearing! I had no clue where to begin. Time to call Mom.

"Hey sweetie! How was the trip to Cancun? How's Vergil? How is the magazine going?" she asked, her words all tumbling over each other.

"Mom, I know you are extremely happy to hear from me, but one step at a time, please," I laughed.

"I know, baby. I just miss you, is all," she said.

"Well, since you asked, the trip to Cancun was absolutely amazing. I miss the girls already. Vergil is here in New York now. He and his business partner are opening their own medical clinic, and we're getting ready to launch the next issue of Enterprise 25 in two weeks," I said.

I placed the phone on speaker and walked over to the counter to grab a glass of wine. My mom's voice echoed through the phone.

"Aw, baby. You just don't know how proud I am of you. You have come a long way. Now, I've already begun putting some stuff together for the wedding. Since you all agreed to do it here in St. Louis, we've already solidified a date, January 21. Is that okay? The church has a reception area as well, so we won't have to pay for two separate locations. Have you begun thinking about color schemes, who you want to invite, your maid of honor, if you want kids at the reception, if you want open bar . . ."

"Mom, please! Slow down!" I laughed. "One thing at a time."

My mom was going on and on about all of this stuff for the wedding, and it just put me in overwhelm.

"Do you think you could just email all of that to me?" I asked.

"Sure, baby, but make sure you let me know what colors you want so I can start looking for centerpieces."

My mom laughed, and we said we loved each other, then ended the call. I picked up my camera and started going through all the photos from Cancun. I was trying to decide which ones to use for the magazine. I opened up my laptop and began to type the story about the trip, for the travel section.

I was so in the zone that I didn't even hear my cell phone ring. Vergil had called. I finished typing my last thoughts and picked up the phone to dial him back.

I slouched on the couch, feeling tired from the day.

"Hey, baby," said Vergil. "I missed you so much. I wanted to make sure I get over there and spend some quality time with you. I haven't seen you in like a week."

"I know, babe," I said. "I missed you, too. You want to do dinner or something? I could eat."

"That sounds fantastic. I'll be there in thirty."

I took a quick shower and dressed for the night out. The doorbell rang, and I did a last-minute spruce-up before answering.

I swung open the door, and Vergil swept me right off my feet. My sling-back heel fell off of my right foot, and I wrapped my legs around his warm, chocolate body. With one hand, he pushed the door shut.

"Damn, baby, you smell and look so good, I want to eat you," he joked.

He smiled at me with his glistening whites and slid me down onto the couch. Then he planted his knees on the floor beside me and caressed the outside of my legs.

"You make me so happy, baby. I just want you to know that," he said.

"Aw, that's so sweet. You make me happy too. So where did you want to eat?" I asked.

Vergil stood up and stretched his tall body out. He straightened his shirt and walked over to the fridge.

"Babe, you know I'm hardly ever here, so there's like no food in there," I said, flipping on the television.

Vergil held up his index finger and took a call in the other room. Now why did he do that? Was there something he didn't want me to hear? That seemed strange, if I was going to be his wife. I was so tempted to eavesdrop, but the little voice in my head told me to trust my man unless he gave me a reason not to. "Stop this, Monica," I told myself. "You've been burned by men so often that you don't want to trust anyone. You've got to get over that."

Vergil came around the corner and asked me if I was ready to roll out. "I was thinking," he said. "How about instead of going to dinner, we hit the grocery store and I prepare you a meal?"

Well, that sounded fine to me. We headed out and hopped into Vergil's Audi R8. What a cool car! Being a doctor allowed Vergil to splurge in what he liked to call "the lap of luxury." He didn't really have any debt that I knew of, and his business was intact, so why not?

"What would you like for Chef V. Taylor to cook you for dinner tonight?" he asked.

"So I get to put my feet up and watch the chef cook?"

"Yes, baby. And I'll stand in the kitchen with nothing but my apron on. Just for you," he joked.

Vergil pulled into the Whole Foods parking lot. I was starting to open the door to get out, when he put his hand on my shoulder.

"Oh no, my lady," he said. "Let me do the honors. I shall astound you with my gourmet selections. Let it be a surprise."

Vergil got out. He certainly was in a great mood. After he went in the store, I glanced around at the car's gorgeous, plush interior. Vergil had good taste, no doubt about it.

I turned my head to take in the looks of the luxurious back seat. I was surprised to see a mysterious-looking black box setting there. It had a combination lock on it, which seemed odd. What did Vergil have that he needed to hide in a lockbox? I was curious, but knew it was impolite to question him about it.

When he came back to the car, he opened the door and handed me a big bag of groceries. He was right about his gourmet taste. In the bag were whipped cream, strawberries, asparagus, fresh salmon, and an expensive bottle of wine.

"*WHHHOOOOO* I'm about to throw down in the kitchen tonight, baby. You really aren't going to want me to leave after this," he said, leaning over and planting a kiss on my lips.

A woman walked past him with a shopping cart, and Vergil nearly backed into her. "Sorry, ma'am," he said with a grin. "See, real love will have you not paying attention."

The woman smiled, and Vergil told her I made him the happiest man in the world. I was quite embarrassed, but it felt good to have a man be proud enough of me to brag about me.

When we got back to my place, I showed Vergil where everything was, put on some sexy clothing, and sat down on the sofa with my laptop so I could work on the magazine while he cooked.

"Babe, can you turn on some music?" he asked.

"Yes, babe, but it's going to have to be some smooth jazz because you know I can't do my work with all of that other nonsense bumping in the background," I said.

"I know, babe. Jazz is fine."

"I talked to my mom, and she's asking what colors I want to use for the wedding. I was thinking peach and cream. Would you like that?"

Vergil crept in from the kitchen and kissed me on the back of the neck. "Whatever you choose, I'm fine with. You can wear a paper sack and I will still think you're the most beautiful woman in the room," he said.

Vergil had a way with words, and I loved me a man who knew how to cater to his woman.

He went back to the kitchen, and I went to the desk to get a highlighter out of my briefcase. Vergil's jacket had fallen on the floor, and I picked it up. A scrap of paper fell out of the pocket. I didn't mean to do it, but suddenly I was opening the paper to see what it said. "TRICKS 026" was written on it in Vergil's hand. I didn't know what it meant and was just relieved it wasn't some chick's number, so I put the paper back in the pocket and hung the jacket back on the chair.

I cleared my thoughts and began to write again. Vergil came over and placed a delicious plate of food right in front of me.

"This looks great," I said.

After pouring two glasses of wine, he sat down beside me on the couch. We ate, laughed, talked, and kissed. At about 3 a.m., his phone rang. It was a call from the hospital saying they needed him to come in.

"Babe," he said.

"Huh?" I was half-asleep.

"They need me at the hospital, so I've got to go. I'll see you tomorrow." He kissed me on the forehead and left.

The next morning I was back at my office and couldn't stop thinking about what "TRICKS 026" might mean. It gave me a creepy feeling, that word "tricks." I brushed it off and got back to work.

Party Time

19

"All right, everyone. Let's get together in the conference room," I hollered. Everyone scurried to their seats for the meeting. The home girls had arranged a bachelorette party for me in Vegas for the weekend. I just wanted to delegate duties, get the meeting done with, wrap things up, and get out of town.

Andrew, our "love and sex" columnist, raised his hand halfway through the meeting. "Ms. Walker," he said, "I was just wondering, since you're getting ready to embark on a journey of love, might you allow me to do a column on you for the upcoming issue? I could write about your wedding, the honeymoon . . . You wouldn't have to get too personal with me, but it might be a great idea for my next article."

"Andrew, I'm flattered, but I would definitely like to keep that aspect of my life very personal. I suggest you post something in this issue about what you're looking for, and maybe you'll get a reader who also is getting married right now, to offer that portion of her life to you for the story."

"That's a great idea. I'll be sure to do that," he said.

After the meeting, Blake walked me back to my office. "I've been contacted by the book agent of an up-and-coming author," I said, telling Blake her name. "Her book is a bestseller and touted by the New York Times as a great read for young adults seeking inspiration. Why don't you let Andrew get this one since he's looking to be so creative?"

"Do you want me to give it to him now or wait until we're done with this issue?" Blake asked.

"Please wait until next week because I want him to focus on what he needs to get done right now. There'll be a book signing and several scheduled author appearances. I'd like for Andrew to cover some of those, too, so we'll have a full spread on the author."

I left work early that evening. Before I knew it, I was packing and getting ready to head to Vegas for my bachelorette festivities. Vergil and the guys were going to stay in New York and do their own thing, his bachelor party being the same weekend. I had no idea what the girls had planned for me, but I was ready for some action.

That night Katrina called. She said she had booked us a suite at a casino right in the center of the strip so we'd be close to everything. "There's absolutely nothing outside that strip but desert," she said.

I'd never been to Vegas before, so I didn't know what to expect. All I could go off of was what people told me. The old folks call it Sin City, and the young folks just know it as a place to gamble, drink, and have a good time.

As the taxi drove me to the airport, I couldn't believe how fast the time had gone. It was already the third week of January, just a week away from the happiest day ever of a woman's life. Butterflies filled my stomach at the very thought of my wedding day.

My mom had everything planned. About one-hundred-fifty guests would be attending. Vergil was excited as were his family. They loved the fact that he'd selected a girl who pretty much had her own thing going on.

When I arrived at the airport, I learned some flights were delayed due to snow trailing in from the north. I checked the departures board and saw my flight to Vegas was still a go.

I wasn't looking forward to the flight. Planes always feel crowded and germy to me. I had been lucky my last few flights because I sat by people who kept to themselves and stayed out of my space. I especially hated when I sat next to a passenger who wanted to make me their very best friend, when I was just in the mood to sleep. I'd be thinking to myself, *Why can't I just get some rest? I really don't feel like being bothered with the gibberish you're speaking right now."*

Other times, if I was up and hyped about a trip, I had no problem chatting with the person beside me. I met some interesting people that way. Some had even played helpful roles in the starting of my magazine.

This trip, I was in the mood to talk, but the person next to me was in the mood to sleep, so I spent the time reading magazines—something I never have the time to do usually. Shortly before we landed, the captain came over the intercom: "Ladies and gentlemen, we are twenty-five minutes outside the great city of Las Vegas. I hope you all brought your smart thinking caps with you." The cabin burst into laughter.

"Gamble wisely and party like a rock star, but keep the drinking to a minimum. Don't forget to check out the great Caesar's Palace. The food is splendid there," the captain said.

When I got off the plane, I headed for ground transportation and opened my phone to see where the girls were. Then it appeared! A big, long, pink limo that had "Bride-to-Be" streamed across the doors. The windows dropped, and my girls screamed out for me to come and join them. I climbed in, laughing.

"Hey, girl, how was your flight!? Gosh, we had an hour delay in the airport, but it feels so good for us to all be together again," Ashley said.

"I know, right? The flight was a little crowded, but you know me and flights don't get along," I said.

The girls shifted to the other side of the limo. Presents were pouring out from under and over the seats. Champagne glasses glistened from their holders, and the Moet bottles were sweating from the ice they were being chilled on.

"Girl, we are going to have so much fun. Now before we get to the hotel, lets pop open one of these bottles and get this party started right," Stephanie said.

She and Ashley were always down for some good old fun. They were both very smart, intelligent, and well-put-together women, but honey, when it was time for us girls to do our thing, they surely knew how to make us the center of attention everywhere we went.

Katrina was more like me. She could party when she wanted, but we both had done lots of goofing around in college, so wild events kind of got played out and old once we graduated.

Ashley passed around the glasses, and Stephanie filled each one the moment they slid into our hands.

"Monica-boo, this is to you," Katrina said. "You are probably one of the sweetest women we know. You are smart, sassy, business-minded, and I'm sure each of us can agree equally: you are strong. You have been through so much in your life. God has blessed you to be courageous yet humble. You have achieved more then you probably could have asked for, and now you've got a man that would walk to the ends of the earth for you. However, this weekend we are turning the hell up, and remember what happens in Vegas stays in Vegas. Monica, we love you. Peace and blessings," Katrina said.

The girls and I all yelled "aw" at the same time, and crowded one another with hugs and kisses.

"Damn, Katrina, did you like write that speech and memorize it? Because that was pretty good. You should win an Oscar, because that was quite a show you put on for us just now," Ashley said.

Katrina playfully slapped Ashley on the arm, and we continued to sip from our glasses.

"Yeah, Monica, you mean the world to us," Stephanie said. "Our circle would not be complete if you weren't in it. We love you, girl, and congrats."

We had another "aw" moment again. Upon our last group hug, the limo pulled in front of the hotel where we'd be staying. The strip was popping as expected, but the weather was a little nippy. Living in New York had me so used to how cold it got up there that this was nothing.

The girls and I started pulling our stuff out of the limo. "How the heck are we going to get all of these gift bags up to our rooms?" I asked.

"Girl, don't worry about it," said Ashley. "We'll just ask some hotel staff to help us. That's what they're there for, right?"

We walked into the lobby and approached the check-in counter. Katrina got our keys, and we headed for the elevators. There was an awkward silence as we stood there waiting while a smitten couple made out nearby. The doors slid open, and each of us almost trampled over one another trying to get on.

"Geez, why didn't they just get a room?" Ashley muttered as the elevator door closed.

We rode to the very top floor. When we got off, no one was in sight. Katrina pulled out the keys and led us to our suite.

"Oh my gosh, are you serious? I own a magazine with tons in the bank, and I've never stayed in a room this nice," I said.

Tears rolled down my cheeks as I pulled my suitcase over the marble floors. The room was outlined with crown molding, there was a Jacuzzi right in front of a window that seemed to overlook the entire city, and in the center of my room was a big, red bed with silk drapes and satin sheets. I was in heaven.

"Guys, I can't thank you enough for this. I love it," I said.

There was a knock at the door. It was the hotel staff bringing the million gifts the girls had left in the limo.

"Oh, you guys can come in and just place the bags in the corner over there," Katrina said.

Stephanie slid each person a tip as they walked out. "So what do you all want to do first?" she asked, throwing herself down into a deep-cushioned chair.

"I could use some food. Why don't we get some room service?" Ashley asked.

"That's a great idea," I said. "We definitely need to be eating if ya'll are going to have me drinking this whole trip. Will we have the limo all weekend?"

"Yes, the whole weekend," Katrina said, with a grin.

Ashley and Stephanie walked through some double doors and into another segment of the hotel suite. Katrina and I followed. We passed through a connecting bathroom with a huge tub, marble shower, and double sinks. and a window with views of the city. On the other side of the suite were two huge beds and a decked-out bar and entertainment area.

"This is hot!" I said, excited.

"Yes, girl, it is. So we were thinking we'd go out on the town tonight, gamble a little tomorrow, then tomorrow night we have a surprise for you," Katrina announced.

I was so amped that I had almost lost my appetite.

"Forget it. Why don't we just do room service and relax in these rooms?" I suggested. "I'm a little tired, and it's too damn cold outside. Besides, I have a few things for work to complete." I pulled out my laptop.

"Monica-boo, it's your friggin' bachelorette party weekend!" scolded Stephanie. "Put that laptop away. Work can wait. You are here to celebrate new beginnings and vaca. I'm sure if anything comes up, Blake will be quick to call. You're only here for the weekend, so they should be fine."

I flipped my laptop closed. "You know what? You're absolutely right," I said. "I'll be back in a sec. Order us some food. I'll eat whatever ya'll get."

I walked into the hallway and took out my Blackberry to call and check on Vergil. There was a quiet sitting area in the center of the hall, and no one around, so I sat down.

"Hey, baby," Vergil answered.

"Hey! I finally got in, and, babe, the room we're staying in is so bomb. Have the guys told you about what they have planned for you tomorrow?"

Vergil let out a heavy breath. "Yes, they have. Babe, they'll have me walking around with a chain and ball attached to it, and the ball has the word "Taken" written across the back of it." He laughed.

"That is too funny. Did you work all day today?"

"No, Larry covered most of my shift. He'll be out with us for the rest of the weekend."

"Well, I was calling to check on you. I wanted to get some work done, but the girls have me convinced I can go one weekend without it. I may sneak away a little later tonight to do some writing. Be safe, and I'll talk to you soon."

"All right, baby. Enjoy yourself. Love you."

When I returned to the room, the girls had outdone themselves. There were trays full of food. So much food, I didn't even know where to start.

"We didn't know what you wanted, so we just ordered a variety of things," Ashley said.

"Thank you. This all looks great," I said.

The girls and I grabbed plates and forks, then formed a small line around what looked like a mini-buffet. I chose fruit, yogurt, nuts, eggs, and a small piece of steak.

After we were all full out of our minds, the girls demanded I open my presents. There was lots of sexy lingerie (no surprise), a lacey blue garter for my wedding-day "something blue," bars of expensive European chocolate, and a pair of bride-and-groom crystal champagne glasses for toasting at the reception. All so cool.

We gossiped until everyone got sleepy, then all went to our quarters to sleep. When the girls were out of the room, I snuck my laptop out and emailed Blake to see where we were with the magazine. It was going to print first thing Monday morning.

Looking through my emails, I noticed I hadn't written a poem or journal entry in a while. Life had gotten so fast and crazy that there was barely anytime for *me* anymore. I pulled out my notebook and began writing whatever came to mind:

> *Never in a million years could I envision my life shaping up the way it has. Not with all I've been through. I've been hurt so many times in the past that I've always had this uncertainty about myself. I blamed me for all of my failed relationships and all of the bull crap I allowed myself to endure all those years. I had a broken spirit, and whenever I brought myself to dating again, every man I met, I shut him out in fear of the same ridiculous incidents happening again. Of course, I know every man is not the same. Well, I know that in my brain, but not in my heart. When you've been broken so many times, trust almost becomes obsolete, and it doesn't matter whether you know the person or not. It's kind of like I allowed myself to believe there was no man on earth capable of caring and loving a woman the way she should be loved. I had a wall up around my heart so thick, there was no way anyone was breaking through. And not only that, but I had it guarded with the most vicious pit bulls. Well, that was until I met Vergil . . . again. There is just this warmth and comfort about him. This connection is stronger than any other I've ever felt with anyone. He makes me feel safe . . . and like I can just completely love openheartedly and not worry about getting shocked by touching some invisible electric fence. This is the way love is supposed to go. Even when I was still dating, I learned very fast that I did not want a relationship where I'd feel like there could always be another woman. If a woman is capable of controlling her tendencies to want to venture out, then a man can do the same, despite their*

so-called "genetic make-up." I feel so alive with Vergil, and I'm hoping and praying that he does right by me. My love for myself is proving to me that it's okay to love and to fall hard into it. Life is too short to settle for anything less.

A poem that I had written a few years ago rang out in my mind, and I added it to the journal:

Ranting, raving, pacing . . .

Waiting impatiently . . .

On love

Does it exist? What does it feel like and how do I know if I've arrived . . . there

In love

Is it tense? Is it tight? Is it something that can be seen through human eyesight . . .

Does it hurt?

Love

Is it covered in beauty? Warm as the earth's sun?

Or is it the cool embrace of wind a runner feels on his run?

Love

Laughing, lusting touch . . .

Waiting patiently . . .

On love

Some real love

It exists.

It's being held like the warmth of a fire

It's being understood when no one understands

It's that internal self-love that radiates one's natural beauty off and into the universe AND

In order to feel this love it has to be rehearsed...

Over and over and over . . . again

In the mirror

I love me

I am enough

I am one tough cookie, and I deserve love . . .

Real love, sweet love, sanctified love

I AM LOVE

I lift my hands, close my eyes, and surrender myself to the sky

No more why

Just love

Release.

I put my ink pen and notebook away, and drifted into a deep sleep.

The next morning, everyone slept in. I woke up first and got dressed quickly, ready for wherever the girls were going to taking me. After brunch in the casino hotel, we walked around the strip. The street was a blaze of lights, even in the daytime.

Vegas hummed with exciting energy. It perfectly matched my own excitement—in just another week, I'd be a Mrs. Doctor and Mrs. Vergil Thomas—I really liked the sound of that.

When afternoon rolled around, we played some slots and watched a burlesque show. Everyone felt tired, so we went back to the suite and took naps. When I woke up, it was dark outside, and the girls were excited to take me to their "surprise." After I applied my last accessory, they grabbed my arms, and we headed down to the pink limo.

Katrina popped open another bottle of Moet, and we toasted to a good night. The limo driver sped down the strip and dropped us at Pure Night Club—Coco and Ice T's premier nightclub. When the girls and I walked inside, the line was wrapped around the building!

"Now this is why I'm too damn old to be at somebody's club," Katrina said.

"Yes, girl, this definitely reminds me of the old days when we could drink like fish and party until the wee hours of the morning," Ashley said.

I remembered those days well. In college we were at Midnight Mondays, Tell-all Tuesdays, Wacky Wednesdays, Thirsty Thursdays, Freaky Fridays, Sultry Saturdays and Sanctified and in somebody's church on Sundays.

"Oh, no, that can't be the line," I blurted out over the too-loud music and roaring crowd.

"Yes, that's the line, but no need to worry, ladies. I got us," Katrina said.

We skipped past the overly dressed women and men whose eyeballs were popped so far out of their heads it reminded me of the movie "Mask" with Jim Carey. As we pushed our way toward the entrance, guys were grabbing and howling at anything that had butt and breast.

When we arrived in the front, Katrina approached the bouncer who was manning that portion of the club. They spoke for a moment, and the next thing we knew, Katrina was signaling us to head on in.

"Wow, did you know that guy?" Ashley asked.

"No, I just told him that missy miss back there was getting married and we had a private section already paid for on the inside, so he let us in," Katrina said.

I had no idea how much a section must have cost the ladies, but they were determined to make this trip one to remember, and I was down with that.

When we got inside, a very attractive go-go dancer twirled me around and placed a blindfold over my eyes. I could hear my home girls laughing. I, however, found nothing funny about having to feel in front of me, trying to navigate my way through the darkness.

Someone grabbed my arm and led me through a beaded entryway. I could hear Petey Pablo's "Freek-a-Leek" blasting through the speakers. I was sat down onto a couch, and the blindfold was removed.

"Oh my gosh, what the heck is this?" I asked. In front of me stood four men dressed as police officers. The room was low-lit and very intimate. My girls were standing back, pointing at the guys sculpted packs and bulging manhood.

Stephanie came over and handed me another glass of Moet and landed a kiss on the side of my face. The handsome men surrounded me and began to grind on my legs, arms . . . it was kind of weird, but given the fact that I was kind of buzzed from the drinks, I was enjoying every minute of the male striptease.

"GO Monica, whooo-hoooo!" Ashley yelled from the other side of the room. The ladies were dancing, drinking, and throwing confetti all over everything.

By the end of the night, the girls and I were beyond tired and ready to head back to our home destinations the next day. We fumbled our way to the limo, and the driver drove us back to the hotel. When we arrived, the streets were pretty much clear, and the sun was on its way up.

"I don't know about going to work on Monday, you guys," I said. "Is that really the sun? I had no idea it was that late."

"You mean that early," moaned Stephanie. "Girl, no worries, because you'll probably never get to party like that again—I mean, like ever."

"I know, right? I told ya'll I have no life. You know what my day-to-day is like. There's no time to be out acting foolish. Hell, if I'm ever out until the wee hours it's because I'm locked away in my office doing final touches on an issue of that friggin' magazine," I said.

My words were slurring, and the rest of the girls were holding onto one another trying to make it to the elevator. The concierge peeped over her eyeglasses, watching us weave through the lobby.

When we got inside the elevator, Ashley fell to the floor and closed her eyes.

"Get up off this dirty floor. We're almost there," Stephanie demanded.

"I know, but I'm so tired. I just wanna go to bed. We have to get up in like three hours to catch flights," Ashley mumbled.

Ding! The elevators doors slid open, and the girls and I grabbed Ashley and wobbled to our rooms.

What seemed like three minutes was actually three hours of sleep. I felt like I was just getting deep in when my friggin' alarm began to sound.

"No!" I yelled over the annoying cockle-doodle rooster that rang out from my handset. Two of the girls were already up and ready to go.

"You know, I didn't even go to sleep because I knew I'd be mad as hell," Katrina said.

She came over to my bed and began helping me pack my items into my suitcase. I had the worst headache ever, and my body felt sluggish and sick.

"Ugh, now this is why I don't drink the way I used to. I never did like the way that damn alcohol made me feel," I said.

"You'll be fine. Just take today and tomorrow to rest and nurse yourself back to health. Tuesday you'll be fly-and-fancy Monica again, ready to take on the world," Katrina said.

The girls and I headed down to the lobby, grabbed breakfast, and packed our luggage into the limo heading for the airport. When we got there, we all kissed and said our goodbyes. Katrina and I headed toward the security gates and threw our luggage on the conveyer belt.

"Ma'am, do you have any electronics or liquid items in this bag?" the security guard asked.

"No," I said.

"Please step this way."

As I walked through the checkpoint, I could hear my cell phone ring. When I came out the other side, I could see it was Vergil calling. By the time I got my shoes on and grabbed my belongings, he had already hung up. I called him back.

"Hey, baby! I miss you so much. I know you had a blast out there in Vegas," he said.

I reached for my carry-on and dragged it toward my boarding gate.

"Yes, babe, I did. I'm so tired now. I only got about two hours' sleep. I don't think I'm going into the office tomorrow. I may just work from home and get myself together."

"Definitely do that," Vergil said. "Don't beat yourself up about not going in. You work hard and deserve a little break now and then. The magazine is already out to print right? What is this, issue five or six?"

I flopped down in a chair near our gate, and Katrina went off to get two cups of coffee.

"Issue five, and it goes to press tomorrow," I said. "Now everyone will be working on issue six. I'll be super backed-up on emails."

"You'll be fine. Can't wait to see you."

"So tell me about your bachelor party!"

"That's one night I do not want to remember. You don't want the details, babe, believe me. I just got a page, so I have to get back to work."

"Okay. I miss you."

"Maybe I'll stop by tomorrow, give you some time to rest today," Vergil said.

"They're boarding us now, so I'll text you when we land," I said, ending the call.

Katrina and I were in first class on this flight. I was happy because I didn't have to sit next to an exit row or be disturbed by people constantly getting up and going to the restroom. My home girl and I chatted a while, then Katrina started to doze off. I pulled a fleece blanket around my shoulders and cuddled up to the window. I was on my way home.

Peach and cream, peach and cream—my mom was driving me damn-near crazy with all this damn peach and cream. Those were the colors for the wedding that was to happen in exactly two days in good ole' St. Louis, Missouri. I could hardly wait. Not only was I about to get married to the world's most wonderful doctor, but I was going to get to see all my cousins, aunts and uncles, and friends I hadn't seen in such a long while.

"Monica. Oh, Mah-nee-cah," Blake called.

His voice rang from behind my half-open office door. I clicked out of the page I was working on and looked up at my assistant, who was now completely inside my office.

"Oh, God, what is it now?" I said.

"Well, I'm afraid Nelly canceled on us at the last minute, so now that's an entire six-page spread gone poof," Blake said.

I rolled my eyes and let out a deep sigh.

"Fix it," I said.

"Oh no, not the 'fix-it,' chant," he said. "Look, I know you're stressed about your wedding and all, but we have work to do here."

He quickly changed the tone in his voice when I stood up from my desk.

"All I'm saying is, where the hell are we supposed to get another celebrity feature on such short notice?" Blake knew, as I did, that a cancellation like this three weeks before we went to print was a true emergency. It takes time to line up and develop feature stories—they can't be tossed together overnight.

My mind drew a blank for a few seconds, then a lightbulb switched on in my head so bright I could see the glare on my computer screen.

"You know what, Blake? I want us to take a completely different approach with this issue. I know readers probably get sick and tired of magazines reporting on the same old fashionable things—millionaire hip-hop moguls and producers who don't have substance other than their ability to make music, sleep with a million women, and blow money at sweaty strip-joints. Look, we can make a difference here. We can maybe even start a trend. We now have the back section where we highlight foster youths and kids that come from challenging backgrounds, but let's dare to be different in this issue," I said. "Let's blow that theme out of the water."

Blake looked as if his face was bound to hit the floor at any second. "Look, boss lady, no disrespect, but have you lost your marbles?"

"Excuse me? You know what Blake, you are really trying me today," I said.

Blake took a seat in the chair in front of my desk, and in walked Veronica.

"Sorry to intrude but you have a call on line one," she said.

"Would you take a message, and I'll call them back when we're done here."

"But it's your mom, and she says it's important. It has to do with the wedding," Veronica said with a grim smile.

"Okay. Put her through."

I picked up the phone and brought my finger to my lips, signaling Blake to stay quiet.

"Yes, Ma, make it quick because I have to get back to work."

"Well, I was just at the grocery store, and do you remember Geraldine, Frankie's daughter?" Mom asked.

I rolled my eyes to the ceiling and Blake covered his mouth in hopes of covering his high-pitched laugh. I brought my finger my lips again, but this time quicker than before. Mom was still talking.

"Ma, come on. Let's get to the climax of the story. I have to get back to work!"

"Well, Geraldine and I had a nice long conversation, and it turns out she knows Vergil through a mutual friend. She said he was a little slickster with a bad rap sheet. Now, you know I'm too old for all that gossiping and stuff, so I didn't want to hear any more of it. I just told her that Vergil and you are happy and due to get married soon and went on about my day, but that was it, baby. Call me when you get home this evening. I got to get these groceries in the house now," she said.

As soon as we ended the call, my stomach tied into a knot.

"Are you okay, Monica? Is there something wrong?" Blake asked.

I was thinking back to the moments of when Vergil and Larry where so secretive when Vergil had first arrived in New York, and that strange note in his pocket, and the night I found him searching through my drawers. Yes, something felt wrong, but I didn't want to air my personal business in front of an employee.

"No, everything is, uh, fine," I said.

"Are you sure? Because you don't look so well."

"I'm fine," I lied. I struggled to get my thoughts back together. This business about Vergil had to wait.

"Now, as for the next issue . . . I want to focus the entire thing on local youth— their accomplishments and their challenges. We don't want to just focus on their problems but on their successes as well. We'll highlight how their failures or disadvantaged situations actually were stepping stones to success. What do you think? I mean, now that I think about it, we need to make it our business to do this once a year. We have twelve issues we can release, so why not make one really worth something?"

I leaned back in my chair, wrapped my hands around the back of my neck and smiled, envisioning the youth issue. Maybe we'd donate the proceeds from it to charity.

"Wow! You know what? I hadn't thought of it that way. I mean, that could be like a form of giving back for you."

"Exactly. So let's cancel all leads for this issue, and let's start rounding up the youth and getting their parents to arrange meetings for them to come in for interviews. Then we'll start cranking out some amazing stories. Sound good?"

"Sounds great, boss lady!" he said.

Blake jumped up from his chair and headed out to spread the news to the staff. As for me, I was packing up my things to head for home. There was absolutely too much weighing on me to focus on work. The wedding was this weekend, and now it seemed possible I was getting ready to marry a man with a bad rap sheet?

I didn't know if I should cry, chalk it up to gossip and ignore it, or call and question Vergil. I didn't have a lick of proof to go on.

When I got home, I pulled out my journal, a bottle of wine, and sat down. *Oh, forget the damn wine,* I thought to myself. *"If I take out a bottle every time I have a problem, pretty soon I'll be a damn alcoholic."* Reluctantly, I put the wine back into the cabinet. But lord, did I ever feel like I needed a drink.

I picked up my journal to write, to sort out the confusion in my aching head, but for once the words wouldn't come. The phone rang from across the room. By the time I got over to answer it, the voicemail had picked up. It was Vergil:

'Hey, baby. Just checking in. I hope you had a beautiful day. I'm so beyond-words excited about our wedding on Saturday. Can't wait to see you this evening. I'll be by as soon as I can get away. Call me if you need anything."

The dial tone beeped and ended the message. I threw myself down on the sofa, crossed my arms over my face, and let out a deep cry.

I hadn't cried in a really long time. Tonight it was all coming out—all the pent-up anxiety. I felt like I was carrying the weight of the world on my shoulders, and didn't have a place to unload it on.

After sobbing for several minutes, I dried my face and turned to a blank page in my notebook. A tear trickled down and left a smear mark on the paper. My pen touched down, and I began to write:

Lost in Love

I have my career and seemingly the world at my feet,

But finding true love is damn-near like pulling teeth.

My support system is strong, and so am I.

So what is it making me sit here, wanting to get rip-roaring drunk and just cry?

There is no good reason to explain why I feel so betrayed. I don't even know if what I heard was true!

That's when I say to myself, "Go to the mirror and look deeper inside of you . . .

How do you feel? What do you believe?

Do you want to leave?

To base your decision for leaving the possible love of your life on some hearsay?

To spend another moment watching your young years slip away?

Or will you trust your gut and say "I do" and go on living life abundantly?

Free?

I threw the tablet along with my pen against the wall. Next thing I knew, I was curled up and passed out on the couch, and a loud knocking noise was coming from the front door. It was pitch-black out, and when I looked at the time, it was after one in the morning.

"Who the hell is it?" I yelled.

I usually didn't like it when people came over to my place unannounced. I definitely didn't like the fact that it was so late.

"It's Vergil, baby. Open the door."

I opened the door and silently let him come in.

"Hey, are you okay? Did you forget I was coming by tonight?" he asked.

I burst into tears, and Vergil ran to my side to comfort me.

"I don't know if I want to get married anymore. It's so—soo hard," I stammered. I was stumbling over the words. My face was so swollen, I could barely see from all the crying I'd been doing.

"Look, baby, it's okay to have cold feet. This is different for you and me. There's so much pressure and stuff to get done—I get that. Hell, I wish I could be here more helping out, but my crazy schedule just won't permit it. You know I'm here for you, Monica, and you don't have to be afraid because I'm going to hold your hand every step of the way."

"It's not that, Vergil," I said. I now had snot dripping from my nose. Vergil went in the bathroom and brought back a box of tissues, then guided me to sit on the couch. He sat down beside me, as I blew my nose.

"Then what's upsetting you, babe? Tell me about it."

"I got a call today that disclosed some unpleasant stuff about you," I said, looking at him out of the corner of my eye.

"Look, I don't want to even know what it is. You know people who are unhappy with their own lives, and possibly want what you have, are always going to be there to throw you off your game any chance they can get. Look at us. I'm a successful doctor; you own your own magazine. Who wouldn't envy that?"

Without saying another word, I put my head in Vergil's lap and let him massage me back to sleep.

When I awoke on the couch the next morning, Vergil was gone, and I felt rejuvenated. I pulled out my big wedding binder and started calling around to make sure everything was set to go. My mom and a few of my aunts had been doing the bulk of the planning, so I knew I was in good hands.

The rumor my mother had told me had greatly upset me, but I had decided I would not be beaten down by negative gossip. I trusted the man I loved. I would stand by him. No man had ever been as sweet and considerate of me as Vergil. It was just impossible that he was a fraud. For once I knew I had the real thing, and I was determined to keep it.

I checked the reservation for my flight. In just two days, I'd be walking down the aisle single and coming back out the door as someone's Mrs.

I Do

21

I was at the office before it opened on Friday, helping Blake wrap up assignments for the youth issue. I was so excited to finally be part of something that was going to serve a great cause. It would not only be good for the youth in the community; it would also show people how they could chip in and help.

"Hey, boss lady," a voice from behind me said.

"Oh my, you startled me. I didn't know anyone else was here this early."

It was Veronica. She had come in early to get a head start on her articles. She was so hands-on when it came to this sort of thing, and her articles in the advocacy section showed what she was made of.

"You know, I really appreciate what you bring to the team, Veronica," I said. "This whole focus on youth was originally your idea."

"Thank you, Monica. But you get most of the credit. Congrats again on your wedding. Will you be back on Monday?"

"I will. My fiancé can't be away from his hospital for long, so we have to put off the honeymoon for a while."

"Have you decided on a honeymoon destination yet?"

That was the furthest thing on Vergil's and my list. He was trying to get the med biz off the ground, and I was too busy to leave the office for more than a few days at a time.

"We haven't really thought that far yet," I said.

"Well, I have a time share in Puerto Vallarta, and you guys are free to use it if you'd like. It goes to waste most of the year."

"Well, that's very thoughtful of you, Veronica. Thanks so much for the offer. I will let you know."

A few moments later, I was on my home to pack. When I arrived, there were roses on my welcome mat. Vergil wanted me to know he was thinking of me.

I entered and threw my briefcase onto the kitchen table. My suitcase lay open and empty. I was supposed to pack it a few nights before; I just had too much on my brain. Those negative thoughts were lingering, but I dared not let them ruin my wedding day.

Even though I was scared as hell and didn't know what to expect when I arrived in St. Louis, I was optimistic and wanted to stay that way. I hadn't told the girls the rumor my mother had heard because it wouldn't do, at this late date, to have friends and family thinking there was something to be concerned about. I had committed to this marriage, and I was going through with it. I trusted my man.

I began to throw undergarments, make-up, and toiletry items into the empty suitcase. I paced back and forth across the living room, trying to think of what else I could possibly need.

I grabbed a few outfits, my perfume, and called it done. *Hell, whatever I forget I'll just have to get it when I get there,* I thought.

My cell rang as I closed the suitcase. I was going to be late for the plane if I didn't get my butt out of there. I answered the phone with annoyance. It was my mom.

"Baby, are you okay?"

"Yeah, I'm sorry. I'm just really tired and I have to be at the airport in like an hour and a half," I said.

"Well, I won't keep you long. I just wanted to make sure everything is good."

"Yes, Mom. Is everything scheduled for the rehearsal dinner? We're still on with that restaurant tonight?"

"Yes, and now don't you worry your little pretty head," said Mom. "All the girls have confirmed they'll be here, dresses are together, your dress is here, and Vergil has his guys set up. You are good to go!"

I was so happy that my mother was the wedding planner. There was no way in hell I could have put together a wedding. I didn't have the time or the patience.

I headed for the train to the airport. When I got to my gate, they were just five minutes from boarding. I saw there was a missed call from Vergil, but I didn't have time to call back.

When the plane took off, my thoughts again turned to my upcoming marriage. Maybe this time in the air would give me a chance to think. I knew Vergil was the man for me. It was this powerful feeling that I hadn't felt for any man in years, and for some reason I felt it for him. His tone made me melt. His kisses made me quiver. His caring remarks kept me wanting more. And as I'd always wanted, when I was in this man's arms, it felt like the warmth of a fire feels on a cold winter's night, or a cup of sweet tea before bed. Vergil loved me. He was my other half.

I dozed off to sleep and awoke to a loud thumping noise and a side-shift in the plane. I was home again . . . back in St. Louis, getting ready to marry the man of my dreams.

As I exited the ground transportation doors, I saw my mom and a few other family members waiting. They were so excited to see me; I dropped my luggage at the sudden lunge of a hug from my Aunt Wanda. She was one of my favorite aunts—always so sweet and down to earth when it came to discussing matters of the heart.

"Sweetie, it's so good to see you! You haven't been back in too long a while." she said, patting my back as she held me. "We are all so happy for you and Vergil. Is that the only suitcase you have?"

"Yes, that's it! We're leaving right back out Sunday, so I didn't need much," I said. I went over to give my mom a kiss. She just grabbed my face and smiled. "Aw, come on, Ma. Don't make me cry," I said.

"I know, sweetie. I'm just so happy for you. I know you've been waiting for this special day for a very long time, and it's finally here."

"Yes, Ma. It's finally here. Well, come on, let's get going, because I'm starved and we've got a wedding rehearsal in a few hours," I said.

As we drove down Lindbergh en route to Highway 70, a dozen memories entered my mind. I thought about my old high school and the great times I'd had there . . .

When we pulled up to my mom's place, several parked cars were outside. Mom opened the door, and a big roar of "Surprise!" rang out over the living room. All of my aunts and uncles, sisters, home girls and cousins were there to greet me.

"Wow, this is amazing!" I said. "Thank you all so much for being here to support me." I was so happy to be surrounded by so many family and friends. Only on rare occasions could we get everyone together like that.

When I walked around the corner and into the kitchen, I saw catfish nuggets, spaghetti, macaroni and cheese . . . I mean the works.

The family conversed and snacked for a while, then loaded the cars to head over to the rehearsal. When we got to the church, everything was absolutely gorgeous. It looked like a dream come true. Peach-and-cream ribbons graced the pews, and the flowers on the altar were staggering in their beauty. There were candelabra everywhere, but those would not be lit until tomorrow.

"Man, ya'll really hooked this place up!" I said.

"You like it?" Mom asked.

"I absolutely love this," I said.

The groom is normally part of the wedding rehearsal, but Vergil couldn't get away from the hospital, so he and his groomsmen wouldn't arrive til tomorrow. The bridesmaids lined up, and we all pranced down the aisle as if it were the real deal. I was walking down the aisle to the traditional wedding song, since I didn't get a chance to pick particular music. We rehearsed for about an hour, then the wedding party drove to our family's favorite restaurant, where the rehearsal dinner was to be held. The atmosphere was dark and intimate, which caused all our voices to be hushed. But there was laughter and toasting in spite of that.

Then the Mom, Aunt Wanda, the girls, and I headed back to Mom's place to prepare for the next day. My dress had arrived, and it was still in the plastic.

"Ma, did you see the dress yet?" I asked.

"Yes, baby. You're going to kill it tomorrow."

"Since when did you start talking so hip?"

"I've been hip since you were born. Now try on the dress. We need to make sure everything fits."

With my short height of only four-eleven and my size-two body, it has always been a challenge finding clothes that fit me just right. But the dress fit perfect. It was a beautiful snow white with a long train that attached to the back. The front was short, about knee-length, and the collar came to my collar bone. The front was plain-Jane but the back was cut into a low V, with pearls stitched along the seams of the V.

I walked out into the living room to get my heels.

"Oh, my God! You look like an angel," my mom screeched.

My friends were completely speechless as well. I twirled in the dress as if I were the character Kim from the movie "Edward Scissorhands." There was a scene where sculpted ice was raining down as if it were snow. Kim lifted her hands and head to the sky, as she smiled and twirled, as if heaven was coming down on her. She was submerged in the essence of love. That's how I felt at that very moment. I was so excited to be marrying the man of my dreams, my best friend.

After all of the crazy hooting and hollering about how beautiful the dress was, I slipped it off and got back into my normal clothes. "So Monica, now that you're getting ready to be a married woman, does that mean no more girls trips?" Ashley asked.

"No, I think we'll still have little weekend getaways. I gotta make the man miss me sometimes," I said, and everyone laughed.

"I remember when I first got married to my second husband," said Katrina. "That was the happiest day of my life. We've been married three years now, and not a day goes by I don't fall in love with him all over again. You got to keep it fresh, Monica. You remember that, honey, because marriage is a real rollercoaster ride."

Katrina had been married before to a man she never talked about. None of us even knew who the guy was. I was just happy she had finally found someone who completed her. That's how it was supposed to be.

"Do you know how you're getting your hair?" Stephanie asked.

"I'm going to do a really funky up-do with some curls. I'm wearing a tiara instead of a veil. Aunt Wanda is lending me my 'something borrowed.' It's these gorgeous pearl earrings," I said, holding them up to show the girls.

"Lovely. Well, what's your something new and old?" Ashley asked.

"I think for my old item, my mom has a broach for me to attach to the back of the dress. You know where the dip is? Right there, I'm going to pin it. And for something new, I got the tiara."

"Cool, cute, and simple," said Ashley.

It had gotten late, and Mom warmed up some leftovers for the girls and me. We ate like pigs and enjoyed a little wine and a movie before heading off to bed.

I missed Vergil so much. It felt like we hadn't spoken in ages. The girls and I made our pallets on the floor in the living room and were out like lights as soon as our heads hit the pillow.

The next morning, my mom had breakfast ready. I was an absolute nervous wreck.

"Good morning, ladies," Mom said as the girls and I strolled into the kitchen.

"Hey," we all said in unison.

"It's the big day. Are you excited?" Aunt Wanda asked.

"I have a million nerves palpitating right now," I said, "but I'm ready."

"Oh, don't worry about that, baby," Mom said. "It's normal to have jitters on your wedding day. Now you all eat up, or you'll be late for your hair salon appointments. "

The girls and I stuffed our faces and showered for the big day. When we arrived at the salon, my old stylist, Latise, was waiting for me. She had been doing my hair since I was a kid. She twirled me around to see how grown I'd gotten. I introduced her to my girls.

"Well, it's a pleasure meeting your bridesmaids," she said. "Rene, Lavonne, and Inez will be doing your hair, ladies." The other stylists stepped forward with a smile.

After about an hour, we were done, dolled up, and pretty. "My hair is banging. Thanks, Latise," I said. "You never let me down."

"Don't forget to send me pictures. Congrats again! Nice meeting you ladies," Latise called across the salon as we all waved goodbye.

Back to Mom's house we went to do make-up and get dressed. The florist had just delivered the bridal bouquets, and the house smelled like a rose garden.

With all the attention everyone was giving me, I felt like I a Hollywood actress getting ready for the set. "I'm so nervous. My hands are sweating, and my heart is racing," I said.

"Don't worry, girl, you'll be fine. I felt the same way on my wedding day," Katrina said.

The girls were nearly dressed, and I was still getting my make-up done. Their peach dresses looked absolutely stunning.

After my dress and shoes were on, Mom came in and pinned the broach on the back of the dress. I put the earrings on, and Mom secured the tiara to my hair.

"Baby, I'm so proud of you," she said. "I have prayed for God to bless your union. Your dad is out in the front, and he's ready to drive you to the church and take you down the aisle."

For the first time ever, I was happy to see my biological father. I'd always wished to be Daddy's little girl. I missed the walks to school with him and the threats to my dates that we had never had. Although I'd always wished I had him in my life to fill that void, I was happy he was finally stepping up to the plate to do his job, and that was to be my father. That was to see me down the aisle and give me away to the love of my life.

When we arrived at the church, it was decked out even more fully than the previous evening. A long white runner ran down the length of the center aisle, and the stained-glass windows glowed in the lamps and candlelight. When the music began, Dad walked me down the aisle. Vergil stood at the altar, beaming at me proudly. He looked ready to wrap me in his arms. He was so handsome, and so were his groomsmen. Tears started to trickle down my face as my dad kissed me on the cheek and handed me off to Vergil.

"You look beautiful, baby," Vergil whispered just before the pastor began.

"We have met here today to witness the joining of Monica Raschell Walker and Vergil Terrance Taylor in marriage. Is there anyone present who has reason to believe these two should not be married?" the pastor asked.

At that, there was a muffled screech from behind me. I turned and saw Katrina with her hand over her mouth, looking like she was going to die. I had no clue what was wrong with her.

"Did one of you ladies have something to say?" the pastor asked, glancing toward the bridesmaids.

There was no reply.

"Well, then. We shall proceed. Vergil Terrance Taylor, do you take Monica Raschell Walker to be your lawful and wedded wife from this day forward until death do you part?"

Vergil replied with an eager "yes." The pastor asked the same of me, and I answered "I do." We exchanged our beautiful rings and stared into each other's eyes.

"I now pronounce you man and wife. Vergil, you may kiss your beautiful bride."

We kissed and turned toward the congregation. Everyone stood, and the music played triumphantly.

The reception, which was in the church basement, was so much fun. Everyone had to congratulate us, and my cheek muscles hurt from so much smiling.

"Can I get the beautiful bride and groom out on the floor?" asked the DJ. "We now will have the first dance."

Vergil grabbed my hand and led me to the floor. He wrapped his hands around my waist, and tears started brimming in my eyes. I was so happy and in love.

"Don't cry, baby," he said, taking his index finger and wiping a single tear from my face. He pulled me in closer and led me all around the dance floor. I closed my eyes and trusted that he'd carry me for the entirety of the song. "Always and Forever," by Heatwave, played through the speakers.

While we danced, though, all I could think about was what my mom once told me, how she never had the chance to walk down the aisle because my father had never divorced his first wife. I was happy to be breaking a generational curse in the family and doing things the right way.

After the dance, I noticed there was no sign of Katrina or Stephanie. It seemed they'd been gone for a while. I stepped over to Ashley's table.

"Have you seen Katrina and Stephanie?"

She shrugged her shoulders and continued conversing with the man who was sitting beside her. Before I could walk away, she grabbed my arm. "Did something happen?" she asked.

"I don't know. I just saw them get up and leave."

"Don't worry your pretty little face," she said. "Go back to your hubby, and I'll find them."

22

The wedding was finally over, and I was back in New York, ready to take on the unthinkable. I was now a married woman, and life was feeling pretty good! I had my man now, my career, family, and great friends. I guessed next would be a little mini-me running around driving us all crazy. But for now I was enjoying life and living it the only way I knew how.

Vergil was back at work, and so I was I. The youth issue was almost ready to go to print.

"Hey, Monica, the pictures from the wedding were absolutely gorgeous!" Blake smiled, air-snapping his fingers twice, as if he were clicking a camera. He was so mushy when it came to marriages and things of that nature.

"Thanks. I'm glad to be back as well, only now as a married woman," I said.

I held up my hand and showed Blake my new wedding ring. It was dazzling, studded with diamonds.

"Oh my, well. Vergil sure has taste. You must have been doing something right to get a man to buy you something as beautiful as that," he joked.

"Hush up. I've earned these rocks, all right. Fair and square, to be exact. I've done pretty much everything I need to do in life, and I'd say I've been pretty decent and honest with others, so this is just God's way of blessing me in return," I said.

"So what did you think of the proofs?" he said, pulling a chair up in front of my desk.

"They look great! I'll read them carefully later, but I don't foresee any problems."

"Sure, boss lady. Just make sure you don't stay too late. I'm sure the mister will be eagerly awaiting his lady's return."

Blake was right. I missed my man, and I couldn't wait to get home and indulge in married bliss. I was longing to feel Vergil's strong, chocolate arms wrapped around me. The thought of him made me smile.

I looked over the proofs and approved them for the issue. I emailed Blake and told him we were set to go.

After I returned home, there was a missed call from Ashley on my cell. I didn't hear it ring because I had it on silence.

Vergil was still at his office—and me, I was tired. I slumped down onto the couch as I always did when I got home. I clicked on the television and dialed Ashley back.

"I noticed I had a missed call from you so I was just returning. What's going on?" I asked.

"There's too much to even know where to start. So Royce had the audacity to ask me if one of his home girls from back in the day could crash at our place for a few days. Apparently she was just passing through and needed a place to stay," Ashley said.

Royce was Ashley's husband. They had been together for almost two years.

"Wow. I don't know what I'd say to that. Really? A home girl?" I asked.

"Yes, a home girl."

"So what happened? I'm confused."

It always took Ashley hours to get to the climax of the story. I just wanted to know what the hell happened already.

"I agreed to let the chick stay for a few days. Royce decides he's going to take her out to see the city. I tell him okay, and they go off."

"Wait. You mean to tell me you let your man go someplace with another chick by himself?"

"Yes, I mean I trust him, and nothing happened anyway. Royce can't lie straight if his life depended on it. So basically they went out and saw the town. They came home, and I had dinner and a few friends over. We decided to play some spades and sip on a few drinks. Royce's 'home girl' got so drunk, she couldn't even walk straight. She then started going off about how she needed to leave and all this other bull, so we let her."

I couldn't believe what I was hearing. There was no way in hell, I would *EVER* trust some random chick I'd never met or even heard of to come and stay in my house with my man there. Not only would she not be staying, he wouldn't be taking her on no drives around the city, either. I would have been pointing that trick in the nearest direction of a motel.

"So what happened after she left?" I asked.

"Well, we couldn't talk her out of it, so off she went! She grabbed all her stuff and drove off. Just an hour ago, Royce got a call. She smacked into another car and banged herself up pretty bad. This chick didn't have a license, and there wasn't any insurance on the car. Come to find out, she's not even approved to live in the U.S."

"Girl, shut-up. I can't believe Royce had some fugitive staying up in ya'll's spot," I said.

Ashley laughed. "I don't know what the hell is wrong with that man. I will never do something like that again. I don't care if it's a family member. They need to find someplace else to stay because they won't be able to stay here."

"I'm still tripping off the fact you let some random chick stay at your house," I said.

"Boo, I have nothing to be insecure about. I think Royce has learned that I will leave his ass at the drop of a dime. Chile, he ain't stupid."

"Okay, honey. Well, I hope you'll get that madness figured out. My man is coming home soon, and I want to have a nice dinner ready for him, so I'll talk to you later."

"Oh, whatever. Way to rub it in. We all know you got you some fine chocolate over there," Ashley said.

I hung up the phone and got up to see what I could fix for dinner. "I can make tilapia, pasta salad, and a fruit bowl," I said to myself out loud.

Vergil and I had this thing of wanting to eat and live a little healthier. Neither one of us really had bad diets; it was just time to retire the New York-style pizza.

Vergil had moved in with me after the wedding, so his stuff was still all over my place. While waiting for the fish to bake, I started hanging up some of his clothes in the guestroom closet. After the medical business was fully up and operative, we'd be looking into buying our first house.

I opened up a box that was sitting on the floor. It had "fragile" written all over it. I reached inside and pulled out the same exact black box I'd seen in Vergil's car some time back. The damn thing still had a combo lock on it, so I couldn't open it. I tried Vergil's birthday as the combination, as well as a few other numbers I knew he used for access codes. No luck. For some reason I felt so uneasy about this black box and just had to know what was in it.

A few seconds later, I heard the front door open. I put the box back where I'd found it, and walked into the living room. Vergil was home.

"Hey, baby!" I said.

"Hey!"

I walked into the kitchen to check on the fish, but it still had a ways to go.

"Is everything all right? I heard some rummaging in the back when I came in," he said.

"Oh, I was just hanging up some of your stuff in the guestroom. There's so many boxes back there, I was trampling over everything."

Vergil walked over and landed a kiss on my forehead. I had my lips puckered and my eyes closed, expecting a real kiss, but a forehead kiss was what I got instead. He walked past me and into the guestroom. I went back to the kitchen, dying to know what he was doing in there.

"Baby, you staying for dinner?" I yelled.

"Um, no, sweetie, I have to be back at the office, so can you make it for me to go?"

"Sure. I wish you didn't have to go back."

"I know. Hopefully when Larry and I finish the setup for our business, I won't have to work nearly as much."

Vergil came out of the back room and into the kitchen. He picked me up and carried me into the front room.

"Baby, you know I love you, right? I promise after all of this stuff is over I'm going to take you wherever you want to go for your honeymoon. My treat," he said.

He grabbed my chin and brought my lips close to his. He lifted up my silk dress and rubbed his hands on my back. We flipped over onto the floor and made love until the timer went off in the kitchen.

"Damn, the food is ready," I said.

"That's okay, babe. It can wait."

When I awoke, I jumped up thinking I'd left the food burning in the oven. I ran into the kitchen and everything was put up. There was a plate in the microwave for me and a note.

> *I love you babe. You looked so peaceful, I didn't want to wake you. I've cleaned up for you and left you a plate in the microwave. I appreciate you, beautiful.*
>
> *Vergil*

I went back into the guestroom, and the black box I was so desperately trying to open was no longer there. I didn't even bother to search for it. I knew Vergil had taken it with him. I went to bed that night without eating, just wondering about who the hell I was married to.

23 Revelation

The next day while at work, I couldn't even focus on what I was supposed to be doing. Vergil hadn't come home the night before, I couldn't find his mysterious box, and I felt like our marriage was doomed. Something was terribly wrong. We hadn't even been married a month yet.

I just didn't get it. I mean, what had I done in my lifetime that was so bad? Why was it that every time something good happened there was always a bad incident to follow? Usually the bad incidents involved the men in my life.

I left the office for a while to grab some lunch. On the way down, I ran into Veronica.

"Oh hey, Monica!" she chirped. "Blake's been talking about how beautiful your wedding photos are."

I sure didn't feel like talking about the wedding with Veronica, or anyone. I needed to extract myself.

"I've got to run, Veronica, but if you want to see the photos, I think Blake still has the album in his office. Tell him it's fine for you to look at them."

"Oh, great! I'll see you later."

I walked to the deli down the street and sat and ate my salad in a daze. My life was flashing right before my eyes, and I couldn't stop it.

I didn't know who to trust anymore. What was the story with Vergil? What, for that matter, was the story with Stephanie and Katrina? Every time I'd talked with them since the wedding, their voices sounded phony and strained. Why had they disappeared from the reception for over an hour that day? Why had Katrina suppressed a screech when the reverend asked if anyone knew a reason why Vergil and I shouldn't get married?

I felt like I had nowhere to turn for guidance. Then I remembered God—God, who I thought of so rarely these days, when all had been going so well.

I now turned my thoughts to the Heavenly Father. I closed my eyes for a moment and ignored the fact that I was in a public deli. Frankly, I didn't care. I needed to connect with God, and I needed His help right now.

I pretended like I was alone in the lunch room. I inhaled, and then I exhaled, then mentally began to pray to the one above. I did that for several minutes until my cell phone rang.

"Amen," I said as I picked up the phone to see who was calling.

It was that heifa Katrina. I knew she was hiding something from me, and I was determined to find out what it was.

"Hey, Katrina, what's going on? You must be off work early today," I said.

"I left a little early. Shoot, tomorrow's Friday, and I'm tired," she said.

Katrina was sounding all normal today, like nothing had ever happened. But I wasn't going to let things slide any longer.

"Katrina, we need to talk. I can't do it from here. I'll call you from home," I said, and hung up abruptly.

When I got back to the apartment a couple of hours later, I phoned her back. Katrina started jabbering about who knows what, but I was ready to confront her, so what she was saying was going in one ear and out of the other. Finally, I interrupted her mid-sentence.

"Okay, let's get this over with," I said.

"Get what over with? Is something wrong?"

"It's actually a lot deeper than that," I said.

Katrina took a deep breath and exhaled.

"Okay, I think I need to take a seat for this one," she said.

"Look, Katrina, I really value relationships in my life, and I have been lied to far too many times to deal with any more of it. I know you know something about Vergil, and you're going to tell me what it is. Not only are you going to tell me, but as a friend, you are going to be brutally honest with me. At least spare me my pride and allow me to decide what your consequence should be after I find out whatever it is you all have been hiding from me."

I didn't really know if I was ready to face the truth, but one thing was for sure, I was ready for the dirty laundry to be aired and the healing process to begin if one was needed. I couldn't go on like this not knowing.

"Monica, I really value our friendship, too, and I would never want to do anything to jeopardize that," Katrina said.

"Please just cut the crap. Just get to the thick of it, and we'll deal with the baggage later."

Katrina sat quietly for several seconds. That's when I knew this could end badly.

"So remember my first husband? The guy I never wanted to mention because the marriage had ended so badly. Well, the day of your wedding I realized that Vergil was my ex-husband," she said.

"Are *you* serious? Why the hell would you wait until now to tell me something as life-changing as that? I think I need a drink," I said.

I got up and grabbed the wine bottle from the cabinet. I sat down on the floor, ready to drink right out of the bottle.

Suddenly I was appalled at what I was doing. *Damn it, NO!* I told myself. *You aren't going to pile alcoholism on top of all your other problems. This reach-for-the-booze crap is having to stop.* I angrily slammed the bottle with the back of my hand. It went flying across the room.

I picked up the phone again and broke into tears.

"Why didn't you tell me?" I asked.

"Monica, I didn't know until the wedding, there at the altar. I'd never met Vergil, and you had never mentioned his last name. I couldn't spoil your wedding and tell you then. You were so happy. I thought maybe he'd changed. I was hoping for the best for you."

"That's a sorry excuse if ever I heard one. You let me marry him, knowing who he was! And now he didn't come home last night, and I can tell there are secrets, and something is terribly wrong!"

"I was going to tell you as soon as the time was right. I knew the guy's name was Vergil, but I sure never guessed it was the same Vergil I used to be married to! That's the God-awful truth. I'm so sorry, Monica. You just looked so happy. I didn't want to spoil your special day, or your first weeks of wedding happiness."

I lay limp in the middle of my living room floor. It was as if the world had crashed on top of me and smashed me into a pancake of nothing. I had so many thoughts and emotions running through my body that I was at a complete loss for words.

"Now tell me the rest," I said.

"What's the rest?" Katrina asked.

"You know the rest. The portion of your divorce you never wanted to reveal to me or any of the other girls. What did this man do that was so bad you couldn't even share it with your supposed closest friends?"

I was now sitting up and leaning against the couch, waiting for Katrina to finish her story.

"Vergil literally wiped all my bank accounts clean. He was a no-good, lying--- you know what? I'm a Christian woman, so I won't even go there. But he wiped out everything I had. He was a big-time doctor here in Atlanta, but he had a gambling problem. And Vergil liked to travel. He wasted our money on whores, clubs, and expensive deluxe suites," said Katrina.

She broke down and cried. For some strange reason, a part of me felt sorry for her.

"Katrina, it's okay. We're going to get through this," I said.

"Monica, you don't understand. This man took the financial stability right out from under me. I was so in love that I let that blindside me from what was going on. I felt like a total fool. That's why I could never tell you guys. That's why before I got married again, it took me a really long time to let my guard down. I mean, this man walked around with a black box that had a combination lock on it. One day he left it open, and I found a picture of him and another woman. Apparently he'd wiped out her finances as well. He told me he was starting some huge, online business. I believed him, so I decided to invest, and he took all my money, wasting it on everything but the business. I absolutely lost everything."

When Katrina mentioned that black box, I stopped being able to hear what she was saying. I was freaking out.

"Katrina, I have to call you back. Vergil's been walking around with that same box, and I need to find out what's in it.

"Are you serious? Monica, please be careful," she said.

I hung up the phone and headed for the door. I knew exactly where his deceiving conniving---he wasn't even worth the words.

I grabbed my coat and headed straight for Larry's. Figured he'd probably be hiding there.

24

Confrontation

I sped down the dark streets of New York with nothing but pure rage in my heart. I wasn't really one for confrontation, but I was so pissed that my blood pressure was on high and my heart was pounding. My breath came hard, and the anger was making me sweat.

Even my yoga breathing exercises couldn't ward it off. I didn't get how any human being in their right mind could ever fathom creating a false persona, pretending to be some great person they weren't so they could go out and ruin other people's lives. How could someone be as evil as that? I'd never know the answer.

All I knew was that this was a cruel world of love and war. Women in most areas were outnumbering men, and the three-string rule between a man, a woman, and God was apparently a joke. When I walked down that aisle last month, I meant every word of what I said to that man. How was he repaying me? By possibly having some side-piece and trying to rip me off of all of my hard-earned money. He was weak, and he knew it; a coward even.

I pulled over to the side of the road because I was starting to cry. The tears were clouding my vision, and it was dark out, so I couldn't afford for anything else to happen—like crashing my car.

I wept, thinking about all the men I'd wasted so much energy on, only to end up in the friend zone or worse, hanging around men who promised to someday make me a wife, but years passed, and that day never came. And this time I'd been so anxious to get married that I didn't listen to the warning God had given—the thing Mom's friend had said about Vergil having a rap sheet. Why, oh why, had I not paid attention? Why hadn't I investigated? How hard would it have been to do an online criminal background check? But all I cared about was getting that ring on my finger . . . lying to myself that I was being noble and "true to my man." My mom used to always tell me that people will only do to you what you allow them to do.

I knew there was no coming back from this. This was the ultimate betrayal. And then I remembered that before Vergil betrayed me, I must have betrayed myself. I had ignored the truth that was right in front of me for the sake of having my "dream wedding." It wasn't really Vergil I'd wanted—I didn't even know him. It was being somebody's Mrs., telling myself I had finally arrived. My greed for being married was stronger than my self-protection instinct and my regard for the truth. At that moment, I felt like a worm squirming in my own slime. I felt like I deserved all the bad things that ever had happened to me.

After crying a while, I remembered again to pray. Help from God always came when I remembered to ask for it. Funny how long I could go before thinking to do that. I needed God now more than ever. I needed Him to remove this self-hatred. I needed Him to forgive my stupidity and help me find a way to believe in myself again.

After a few moments of prayer, the intensity of my crying subsided. I could feel God loved me and understood. I never meant to do something wrong. God knew that. I was trying to be a good person. It just was my powerful lust for love that had driven me to it. When, oh when, would I stop seeking love in a man and truly work on finding it in myself? I knew I couldn't have a healthy relationship until I learned to do that. I thought I had learned, but I hadn't. I raced toward the altar like a dehydrated horse toward a bucket of water. Why had I been so desperate? So willing to marry Vergil in spite of all the warnings life had given? It had to be because I had never truly loved myself, after all. I was mouthing the words "I love me," but if I truly did, this marriage would never have happened.

I shifted my clutch and continued to drive. A thousand thoughts were clouding my brain. I was trying to calm myself so I could at least have a lucid conversation with Vergil when I arrived at Larry's.

I turned on the radio, and it was playing gospel music: "Be encouraged, no matter what's going on. He'll make it all right, but ya' gotta stay strong." I hummed that song until I'd finally pulled in front of Larry's place. I took a few deep breaths and stepped out of my vehicle. The music had calmed me down. I don't know what I'd have done if it hadn't.

I should bust the windows out on his car. Maybe even slash all the tires or write "Deceiving Bastard" in red lipstick across the side of his freshly washed white paint. I chuckled at the thought. All that sounded great, but none of it would change the way I was feeling. Plus Larry lived in a nice neighborhood. I didn't want to get arrested and see my name in the paper. There was no way I was ever going to allow something like a relationship to ruin my professional or personal image. But then again, love made a sane person behave in the most insane ways. I'd have to make a point of controlling myself.

I got up to the door and rang the bell twice before a light clicked on from the upstairs window. I could see Larry through the glass-stained frame on the front door, running down the stairs.

He opened the door and stood there for a brief second, wordless.

"Hey, Monica. It's awfully late. I was sound asleep. Is everything okay?"

Part of me was wanting to say sarcastically, "Everything's just fine," while another part wanted to smack his ass down for asking such a stupid question.

"You have a man staying in your house. A man who is newly married and should be at home with his wife, and you ask if everything is okay? Larry, don't fool with me. I know you know what's going on, and that's why Vergil is over here."

I pressed past Larry and walked inside the front door.

"Where is he?"

"Look, Monica, I know you're really upset, but I have my daughter this week, and she's upstairs sound asleep. Can you just keep it down, and I'll go get Vergil?"

I sat down on the big white sofa I once had so admired and waited for Vergil. How many people had been ripped off for Larry to afford to purchase that sofa?

"Hey, baby," Vergil said, coming down the stairs. He sounded innocently tired, like he hadn't done a thing.

"Don't 'hey baby' me. We need to talk, and we need to talk *NOW*," I said.

"Look, you guys can go down to the common room in the basement," said Larry. "It's soundproof because we have our Super Bowl parties down there."

He led us downstairs and asked if we'd like a drink. When neither of us replied, he went back up without a word.

"So what is it that you need to say to me?" I asked. I was so angry I felt like streams of fire were coming out of my eyes.

Vergil sat there like he had nothing to explain, and I just couldn't believe it. The stupid look on his face was making me angrier still.

"Look, I know I haven't necessarily been completely honest about who I am and what my real intentions were for you, but I can explain," he said.

"Explain? I want to see what's in that mysterious black box you've been hiding. Explain to me the whispering conversation between Larry and yourself when you first arrived in New York. As a matter of fact, explain to me what "TRICKS 026" means—the message I found on that note in your pocket. How about you explain to me your marriage with Katrina and why no one ever told me!" I yelled.

Vergil slid down in his seat and pressed his left hand to his forehead.

"Vergil, you've been completely dishonest with me, and I have a right to know the truth."

He stood and went into a back closet and pulled out the black box he'd been trying to keep away from me. He input a code and handed me the open box. I begin to sift through the items with tears rolling down my face.

There was a photo of Vergil with his arms around a pretty black girl, receipts of purchases that were made with my money and were not for the medical business, and a travel brochure for a resort in the Bahamas with a heart-shaped sticky-note attached that read, "How about this spot for our honeymoon, sweetie?" I was enraged.

"You know what? I don't even know what to say. I just have one question. Why did you do this to me?"

"If I had the answer for half the stuff I do in my life, I would tell you, but honestly, I don't have an answer. The truth is that I'm a dishonest and horrible person, and I am so sorry for what I have done to you," he said.

"What was the message on that paper?"

"The password to an offshore bank account. To tell you the truth, I was supposed to wait until we got married, and once I got access to your accounts, I was going to clear them out."

I got up and slapped him across the face.

"What did Larry have to do with this? Is that what y'all were creeping off and whispering about?"

When Vergil didn't answer, I knew for sure that Larry was involved. This two-timing loser and his no-good friend were getting ready to rob me of everything I had saved. I wanted to call the cops and report them, but I'd caught them before they'd committed the crime. I knew the cops could only dismiss it.

"Your stuff will be outside my apartment front door by noon. Have it gone by 5 p.m., or it goes to the dump. I'm getting this marriage annulled. Don't think you and that side-chick of yours are getting a dime of my money. I worked for it, and I'll never let anyone take it from me—especially not a lying, thieving bastard like you."

I was already on my feet, so I headed for the stairs.

"Monica, wait," he said.

I turned around to see what the hell he wanted.

"I'm sorry for what I did to you. I know it was wrong," he said.

"'Sorry?' Bullshit. Save 'sorry' for the cops the day they drag you to prison after the next poor fool you cheat. Hell, prison isn't good enough for you. I'm done here."

I walked out of Larry's house and got into my car feeling like a huge weight had been lifted off my shoulders. The chaos was finally over.

I felt pain in my heart, but I was grateful that I'd been protected by the one above. This could have ended really badly for me.

I was going to be strong and let Vergil go, despite how in love I'd been. I knew now it wasn't him I had loved—it was a fake Vergil, the illusion he'd created of a kind and caring man. None of that caring had meant a damn thing. It had all been a lie, a trick to get me off my guard, to trust him and fall in love, so he could get control over my money. I'd fallen for a man who didn't exist—the man he'd pretended to be.

I drove off into the darkness. In the east, a sliver of silver was showing—the dawn of a new day. Someday I would look at this moment as a lesson learned, a way to develop a better me. But right now I was numb, unable even to cry.

When I got home, I picked up the bottle of wine I had thrown across the room and put it back in the cabinet. In a few hours, I was supposed to be at the office, but work would have to wait. I needed the morning to clear out Vergil's stuff, and I needed the day to cry and pray. And I needed to find a locksmith to change my locks before Vergil came by.

I lay down on my bed, muttered another prayer, and drifted off to sleep before I could even finish.

"Dear Lord, I just want to take the time out and thank You. Not to ask You for much at all, just to say thank You. Thank You for all you have given me, and most of all, thank You for my beautiful angel—Monica, my daughter. I know over the last few years she has gone through some trying times. In the midst of it all, I know that You have protected her and that every trial You have brought her has been for a reason, and for that I thank You, Lord. I ask now that you protect Monica as she travels through life looking to make an impact on the world and that she glorifies Your name while she does it. I ask that you strengthen her as she deals with the emotions of getting over her sham marriage and that you will protect her as she journeys to someday find a new mate. I ask that the new man is covered by Your saving blood, that you equip him with all the tools he needs to do right by my daughter. Until the time comes, I ask that You give Monica the strength that she needs to make it day to day and to wait for your blessings, that she not fall victim to just the first guy she meets, that she takes the proper time to heal and enjoy life. That she tackles and corrects her own faults so that she's open and receptive to receive love when it arrives. We know that we should love and love deeply because it covers a multitude of sins, but let it be real love and not just some false pretense of it. In Jesus name I pray. Amen."

"Mom, that was so sweet of you to call back this early in the morning and pray over my life. I really needed that," I said.

"Let me read you this poem you wrote a few years ago. I'm not sure where you got lost, baby, but this may help you find your way back," said Mom. She began to read:

The heart has two sides

The side that wants what it wants and the side that's fueled and haunted by mistrust

Deep, intimate, and dark frustration

Full of hope yet blinded by the complications . . . of love.

The human body is love

Its very essence can bring the most pleasure or radiate the most pain,

Yet it remains a spiritual entity, forever yearning and desiring completeness

A wholeness that can only be manifested by looking in the nearest mirror and peeking in on the soul.

What are its intentions, and who's holding the reigns to lead it to its goal?'

Love.

One can take its hand and feel the beating of an optimistic heart

But if the two sides are battling one another, the connection between them pulls them apart . . .

Mending the broken heart takes some time, but it can be done

The bringing together of two eccentric sides is a battle won.

It's the realization and the centering of one's self

Loving itself from the inside and radiating a warmth that can surely be felt.

Self-love is the absolute best love . . .

When you can hug yourself and be okay with the loneliness . . . that's love

Sometimes the body misses out on some of the most amazing blessings

Because of its need for instant gratification

But the absolute best is given to the ones who are abundantly patient.

If the grass was greener on the other side, you'd already be mowing it.

I was a sinner and I knew it. Most of the human race was. Now I was no one to judge, but some people just acted as if everything was always right and that they were perfect and never did anything wrong. I was happy to know that I was woman enough to admit my faults, repent, and move on with life. I still wasn't sure why this disaster had happened to me, but I would figure it out. God would show me the way.

"I just wanted to call and give you some sweet words of wisdom, baby. You will be just fine, and you will take care of yourself. Just let me know if you need anything," Mom said.

"Okay, Ma, I'll be fine. Don't you worry about me. Love you, and take care."

The locksmith came and changed the locks within an hour of my call. That afternoon, after crying all morning, I felt like going in to work. I really didn't want to be home when Vergil arrived to get his things. I grabbed my laptop and bag. I didn't know if it was a good or bad idea to go in. What I did know was that I didn't want to stick around the house sulking over an issue that was now completely over.

When I finally got to work, luckily there was barely anyone there. Friday was always lightly staffed, with lots of people pulling 10/4 shifts. This made me glad, because I definitely didn't feel like explaining my personal business to the office.

I rolled up to my desk and entered my password. A knock came over the door.

"Can I come in?" the voice said.

It was Blake. I didn't want to talk to him, but I couldn't just tell him to go away. "Come in," I called.

"Are you okay?" he asked with an alarmed glance, after looking at my face.

"I'm fine. I don't want to talk about it right now."

"I know, Monica, but talking is therapeutic. It breaks my heart to see you looking like that. I'm not asking you to explain what happened, but if you want to talk, just remember I'm here for you."

Suddenly it felt like my heart dropped into my stomach. The bottom half of my body felt heavy, and there was a frog in my throat.

Don't cry, Monica, I thought.

A tear rolled down my face, and I was powerless to stop it. My computer screen blinked to black, and my hands slid down into my lap. Blake got up and walked around my desk to console me.

"You are awesome, Monica. I know I've told you this a million times over, but if I was straight . . ." Blake stopped.

"You know what? This is not who I am," I said.

I stood up from my desk and pumped my arms out. I knew deep-down inside this wasn't going to be an easy feat, but I was ready to take the steps now. I was a business owner, for crying out loud, and my game face always had to be on, no matter what I was going through. I couldn't appear weak to the public. There was work that needed to be done, and I was going to do it.

"Okay, Blake. Show me the last galley of the youth empowerment issue," I said.

I started to look through the pages, and the images made me smile. This issue took me back to when I was a young kid trying to figure out where life would take me. My love life might be a disaster, but my career was right on target. I wanted to show the next generation how they could do it, too—no matter the circumstance.

"Wow, this looks great, Blake. You guys really did your thing on this issue," I said.

"So does that mean we can send this one to print?"

"I'll hand it back first thing tomorrow, and we'll be good to go."

A New Day

I always called Maisy on Sunday mornings—the old lady from St. Louis who encouraged me when I was so lost after breaking up with my old college boy-friend, James. Maisy believed in me when I couldn't believe in myself. I owed her so much.

But after I moved to New York, I told her less and less of what I was thinking and feeling. Our phone chats grew shorter. I was losing my way again—I can see that now. I think I was ashamed to talk about the mistakes I was making. The same part of me that wouldn't investigate the truth about Vergil before the wedding, kept me from telling Maisy what was really going on in my life.

It wasn't that I thought she would judge me. Maisy wasn't like that. But I was closing my eyes to the writing on the wall. And if I told her everything, I'd have to look in the mirror.

Then the divorce happened, and I wanted to come clean. I really needed some good advice. Maybe Maisy could steer me out of the mud my life had gotten stuck in again.

"It's Monica, Maisy. Can you talk?"

Her sweet voice crackled through slight static on the other end of the line one Sunday morning.

"Baby, it's good to hear from you. I always have time to talk to my girl. How is marriage suiting you?"

"It's over, Maisy. My life has turned upside-down. Again! Vergil was a fraud." I told her the whole miserable story. She was quiet for a long while.

"You still there, Maisy?"

"I'm here, baby.

"I thought I had it figured out, you know? I really tried to love and respect myself," I said. "But I think now all I wanted was to get my hands on a wedding ring. I threw all my instincts out the window, I wanted it so bad."

"When you want something that bad, it can run away. It's like holding sand in your hand too tight. It'll slip through the cracks."

"So this means I don't really love myself?"

"I'm thinking you probably do, but loving yourself's just part of it, child. You have to let in the love of the Lord, and other people, too."

"I did kind of forget about praying for a while."

"We're supposed to love God with all our hearts and our neighbor as ourselves," said Maisy.

"So you're saying I don't do that."

"Baby, you know best about that."

"I'm praying again, every day. I guess I love my neighbor, whatever that means."

"Seems to me it means thinking about more than just ourselves and how to get what we want. Means noticing when other folks are down, or needing something. Stepping out of our problems a while and paying attention to what's going on around us. Doing something to help."

"I don't really do that. I've been so busy."

"Well, taking care of yourself is real important, too, child. But the Bible says to take it the rest of the way. Love yourself first, then share that with your neighbor. That fills up the empty spot in your heart like nothing else will."

Maisy gave me a lot to think about. All I'd been focused on for the longest time was somehow finding my man. I wanted to be loved but didn't give much thought to the people around me. Others had hurts inside, too, and probably troubled childhoods. Maybe if I reached out more—would that make a difference?

————*——*——*

It's been a little over a year since my sham marriage ended. After talking with Maisy, I decided to take myself off the market for a while, to try and heal from the inside out. If I was addicted to getting married, maybe I had to take a break from men.

I decided to get personally involved in the cause of foster youth. It's one thing to give kids a magazine cover and some money, another thing to give them your time and attention.

I joined a group called Big Sisters. They linked me up with a twelve-year-old named Jordan. She has a background a lot like mine. I visit her on Saturdays, and take her places she's never been before. She'd never been to the seaside, can you imagine? And with the Atlantic Ocean right next door.

It's fun finding things to do and show her. She seems to look up to me. She sees me as better than I am, and that makes me want to be a better person—wiser, more giving.

No one ever took me to museums when I was little, but I take Jordan. I read up on art, and we went to an art museum. I read up on oceanography, and we went to an aquarium. I found books for her to read about art and ocean life. She got pretty excited. She sees things in a way that makes me smile. I'm smiling a lot more than I have in a long time.

Sometimes we go to concerts. She loves the sound of violins, so I bought her a violin and hired her a teacher. Jordan got really good at playing after she practiced a while. Then I bought a flute for myself, and the teacher gave me flute lessons. Now we gals can do duets together. I can't believe I'm having fun, and without a man in the picture.

The weird thing is, now I feel I have something of value to share with a quality man. Something more than just a sexy body. I have interests, and ideas, and opinions. I can discuss history and composers. I can attract a man who's more than a sex object because now I'm more than a sex object in my own eyes.

I see myself as a woman of substance, someone with a heart and a brain. A giving person—finally—who's learned that you lock yourself in a cage if all you ever think about is your own problems and your own self. It may sound cheesy, but I feel like whole new worlds have opened up to me since I figured that out.

I'm taking an art history Continuing Ed class at the local college. A couple of months ago, I made friends with a classmate. He happens to be a guy, and not bad-looking, though by no means the kind of dude I'd have looked at twice in the past. He's nerdy, but humble and smart. Easy to talk to. Interested in interesting things. He never does the come-on lines I always got from the guys in the bars.

We haven't GONE a date yet, but that's just fine with me. Sunday he went roller-skating in the park with me and Jordan. I'd never been on skates before and ended up in a heap. Jordan and Jed held my hands until I got steady on my feet again.

I don't really know if I'll ever get married. It would be grand, of course, with the right man, but I know now there's more to life than snagging a wedding ring. Been there, done that. The ring by itself isn't worth a damn, let me tell ya'.

I still get together for weekends with the girls. They drink pretty heavy, but I stick to two a night. I sit back and laugh at how silly they can get. They're loyal as dogs and funny as clowns. I'll love them forever. They'll always be my home girls.

But I can see new friends on the horizon, people I share interests with. New interests. There are more things in life than boozing and smooching and having a job that impresses people. I know that now. There's better stuff to do than working yourself to a frazzle, worrying about getting a man, and endlessly telling yourself you're loved and okay.

You have to reach out and grab hold of life, you know? With both hands. Grab hold of its finer things—all the beautiful stuff you miss if you don't slow down and look past yourself and what you think you just *have to* have to make you happy.

I was miles from walking the talk. I had to take myself out of the game for a while. Going a year without dating, without even dressing for a man? One of the best things I ever did—for me.

The change of focus opened my mind and my heart. From where I stand, it looks like a brand new day. And the weather is going to be fine.

About the Author

SERENA KING is a first-time author who has personally lived the challenge of making your way in the world when you're young, female, and black. The child of troubled parents, she grew up in foster homes. The adventures of Monica, her heroine, are based on the writer's life experience.

Serena is an author, blogger, and mentor. She has published content on Yahoo, provided journalistic coverage for the National Association for Black Accountants, and served as staff writer for The Panther Newsletter.

Serena lives and works in Georgia but hails from St. Louis, Missouri, a city filled with history. She is working on her second book, a memoir.

Serena is available for speaking engagements and can be reached at serenarkingbookings@gmail.com. Visit her website at serenarking.com.